THE SANDMAN

by

Geoff Collins

This book is a work of fiction. Names, characters, places and incidents are either the product of the author's imagination or are used fictitiously. Any resemblance to actual persons, living or dead, or to actual events or locales is entirely coincidental.

THE SANDMAN

The publisher does not have any control over and does not assume any responsibility for author or third-party websites or their content.

Front cover designed by Geoff Collins

Front cover art: Shutterstock File ID: 1372247075
Back cover art: Dreamtime File ID: 44795346
Interior art: Badge illustration Shutterstock File ID: 8613001
Interior art: Dog illustration: Pixabay CC0 Creative Commons Free for commercial use
Interior art: Gun illustration: publicdomainvectors.org
Mercy Killings cover: Art by Erick Johnson … www.robertlanestudios.com/erik-johnson

Edited by Joe Gartrell and Ben Gibson of Word Mule. www.wordmule.com

Published by A&J Publishing, LLC
3266 Hartwell Street
Johns Island, SC 29455

Visit the author's website: www.booksbycollins.com\

Categories: FICTION / Thrillers / Crime

ISBN: 978-1-951744-36-6 (eBook)
ISBN: 978-1-951744-37-3 (paperback)

Version 2020.09.04

To my friends at Project Paw Alive and the many other police and military K-9 organizations and support groups.

www.projectpawsalive.org

A special thanks to Joe Gartrell and Ben Gibson of Word Mule.
www.wordmule.com

This book is dedicated to …

All those individuals who work tirelessly in law
enforcement to keep all of us safe and free from harm.

TO SERVE AND PROTECT
LAW ENFORCEMENT
POLICE

BOOKS BY GEOFF COLLINS

Family

Ages 7 - 13

Ages 7 - 13

Ages 8 - 16

Adult Content

Adult Content

Adult Content

Adult Content

Adult Content

Adult Content

Available at:

BARNES & NOBLE
BOOKSELLERS

amazon.com

Nick Giordano Novels

"A Holy City Mystery Artfully Spun"

"Geoff Collins is a wonderfully versatile writer (check out his bibliography), and here, he weaves a delightful mystery set in the Holy City. Hop along and crack this case with Giordano—you won't regret, and it will get you primed for the other books coming along in the series."

"Well Written … Interesting Characters and Plenty of Suspense"

"Good mystery with interesting characters and plenty of suspense. A cybersecurity expert is hired to determine if narcotics theft is taking place at Charleston SC hospital and who is behind it. Well written with lots of fascinating details."

"Wonderfully Crafted Story Set in Charleston"

"Wonderfully crafted story set in Charleston, SC—great story line and vivid imagery. Collins follows Giordano with insight and honesty. Can't wait for Nick's next adventure."

"A Fast and Exciting Read"

"The books are a fast read. Exciting and held my interest throughout. Hope to see more from this author."

"Another Wild Ride"

"Tools of the Trade takes us on another wild ride with Nick Giordano and his crew. Collins, as he did with his previous book in this three-part series, deftly weaves on intricate story line that builds to a satisfying, thrilling end. Highly recommend Collins, a writer who deserves a vast readership."

"Excitement and Suspense"

"Excitement and suspense as mafia and white supremacists fight over the drug market in Charleston SC. Characters well-developed and interesting story line."

"Hopefully More to Come"

"In this series, which sadly wraps here with Book Three, Collins found a higher gear with each, serving up a fresh batch of nasty folks for the series' core characters to root out and take down. That the books were set in Charleston only added to their delight. The only rotten aspect here is that this is the last we'll see of Nick Giordano and his pals—that is, unless, this crew comes around for cameos in one of Collins' future works. Hats off!"

Adam Stone Novels

Book 1

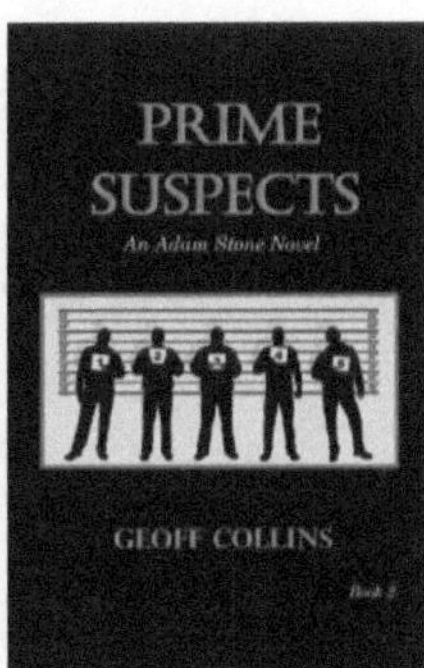

Book 2

Book 3

"Sleep, those little slices of death—how I loathe them."
                                        —Edgar Allan Poe

*To die, to sleep—To sleep, perchance to dream—ay, there's the
rub, For in this sleep of death what dreams may come …*
                                        —William Shakespeare

THE SANDMAN

CHAPTER ONE

DETECTIVES ADAM STONE and Marcus Williams joined their fellow police officers along with local politicians and assorted dignitaries at City Hall for Ed Merchant's swearing-in ceremony as Charleston's new chief of police. Merchant had been a captain on the force for the past eight years and was replacing Dan Taylor, the outgoing chief and a true icon in South Carolina law enforcement. The appointment surprised no one, as there was never any doubt that Merchant would be the new chief once Taylor decided to retire.

Chief Taylor's illustrious career spanned some forty years, the last twenty-four as chief. Marcus joined the department the same year Taylor became chief—Adam became a member of the force a few years later. The two detectives had been partners the last eight years and were part of Captain Merchant's Special Operations Unit.

Merchant's promotion left a captain vacancy, requiring Mayor John Tecklenburg to appoint a successor. To the surprise and disappointment of many officers in the department, Tecklenburg appointed Lieutenant Frank Boyer. Boyer had transferred in from Chicago as a lieutenant on Charleston's force only three short years ago. The disappointment was not only because of his short tenure with the department but also due to a personality that was viewed as arrogant and egotistical. At the risk of being politically incorrect but accurate—Frank Boyer was a horse's ass. It was obvious his appointment was based on politics rather than competence. Even though Boyer had been a lieutenant in the department for the past three years, Adam and Marcus had little if any interface with him. As members of the Special Operations Unit, they had always reported directly to Captain Merchant.

Marcus leaned into Adam and lowered his voice, "Looks like it's official now, Boyer's our new boss. If being an asshole was a crime, Frank would be serving multiple life sentences. This should be fun."

"Yeah, a blast, my friend," Adam responded. "Let's just keep our heads down and see how long he lasts."

Like any organization, the department had its share of bootlickers and ass-kissers who would suck up no matter how inept and autocratic their superiors. Adam and Marcus would take their orders as given but had been professionals too long to play those games. There was no doubt in anyone's mind that they both would have been in line for the captain's position had they not passed on promotions in order to remain on the front lines. Neither of them had the inclination to leave the street. Their tandem work had consistently led the department in closed cases for the past eight years. Their relationship had grown well beyond that of being merely partners—they'd become best of friends in spite of their radically different backgrounds.

Adam was raised in the predominately white, upper middle-class Charleston suburb of Mt. Pleasant, and Marcus in North Charleston's gang-infested Union Heights neighborhood.

Marcus spent much of his youth caught up in the gang culture until his freshman year at North Charleston High School. His unusual size and physique caught the eye of the high school's head football coach. Had it not been for the coach convincing him to try out, he would have most likely ended up a gangbanger. By his senior year, he was six-foot-four and 260 pounds and had earned first-team All-State honors and a full ride to Clemson. Marcus' accolades on the gridiron did not stop there. During his final year in college he was named a second-team All-American linebacker. He was even more proud when he was tapped as an Academic All-American his senior year.

After graduation, he was a late-round draft choice of the Cleveland Browns. He never made the team and eventually took a job with State Farm Insurance. After two tedious years with the company, he joined the Charleston Police Department and began his career in law enforcement.

Adam Stone, at a slim 180 and a shade over 6', demonstrated his own athletic prowess on the basketball court. While never attaining anything near Marcus' level of recognition, he was a four-year starting point guard at Francis Marion University. Although his college days were long gone, he continued to play ball in a highly competitive downtown Charleston league and with a group of his friends on Saturday mornings. He'd lost a few steps over the years but was proud that he could still hold his own against the younger players.

~~~~

The ceremony ended around 4:30 Friday afternoon. The crowd was dispersing when Marcus told Adam he was picking up his wife, Makayla, at the bank for a quick dinner and would see him back at the Lockwood station. This was Adam and Marcus' Station Rotation weekend requiring them to work Friday and Saturday night shifts.

Adam also left and made the drive to Charleston Collegiate School on Johns Island to pick up his fifteen-year-old daughter, Piper. It had been over three years since his wife, Ann, had been brutally murdered at the hands of a serial killer. Adam sold his James Island house after Ann was killed and moved into a three-bedroom, two-bath apartment with Piper. The third bedroom was often used by Tracy Kendall, the mother of Adam's late wife. Since Ann's death, Tracy had become an even more integral part of their lives and would spend nights with Piper when Adam had to work late.
~~~~

Piper, a superior student and excellent athlete, had soccer practice after school until about 5:00. Adam pulled into the roundabout in front of the school's gym and waved to his daughter. It continued to amaze him how she'd grown. It seemed like only yesterday she was just a kid chasing the ball around in the back yard. But now she was on the brink of womanhood—showing a confidence and willingness to take on the challenges that lay ahead. His only regret was that Ann was not here to experience her metamorphosis.

"Hi, Dad," she said as she slid into Adam's Charger. "Can I go to the movies with Chloe tonight? Her mom said she'd drive."

"Sure, Sweetheart. Tracy will be staying at the apartment this weekend. I've got to be at the station, but we can grab a bite to eat at home before I have to leave."

"That's cool," Piper said, "but you work too much, Dad."

Adam smiled and retorted, "Oh, you think so? Just wait until you graduate from college and get a job. Then we'll talk about working too much." Even though Adam dismissed Piper's comment, he often regretted the amount of time his job forced him to spend away from her.

Back at the apartment, they were delighted to find that Tracy had already whipped up dinner. Adam barely had enough time to eat and take Max, their Lab mix and fourth member of the family, for a walk before he had to leave for the Lockwood station.

~~~~
~~~~

Marcus was already at his desk in the bullpen when Adam arrived. Things were normally quiet on the weekend rotations until around 1:00 in the morning, but the patrol officers handled everything unless there was a shooting or some other event that required the attention of the detectives.

Technology had come a long way in improving the efficiency and effectiveness of law enforcement. However, it had yet to replace an officer's cumbersome and time-consuming tradition of submitting paper reports. These weekend assignments were a good time for Adam and Marcus to catch up on that front.

As in most police stations, the coffee sucked, so Marcus left Lockwood about 10:00 to pick up coffee and muffins at The Coffee Cup. As he returned, he passed a latte and muffin to Adam and said, "I need to talk to you about something."

Adam stopped in the middle of taking the top off the latte. "So, talk."

"All right. I'll get right to it. I've been thinking about leaving the force."

The comment came out of left field and caught Adam completely off guard. He set down his coffee and was quiet for a moment, then responded, "Why?"

"Makayla and I have been talking about it since I got hurt. Plus, her dad's restaurant supply business is doing really well, and he's been asking me to come aboard to help out for a while now."

A little over six months ago, Adam and Marcus were working a drug trafficking case when Marcus was attacked and brutally beaten by two men from the Sinaloa Cartel. He suffered a severe concussion, internal injuries, and multiple broken bones. It was touch and go for a time, but he eventually did recover. It took over a month of physical therapy before he was ready to rejoin the department—and even then, he continued to feel the effects of his injuries.

Adam had seen Marcus struggle since the attack, but the thought of him leaving the department never crossed his mind. "I don't know what to say, brother. I know you've been through a hell of a lot since you got hurt, but this is in our blood, man. We bleed blue." Adam waved his arm around the bullpen. "This is what we do."

"I know," Marcus quickly replied. "I already have my twenty-five in and can leave with my full pension and benefits. I don't know how I'll handle life on the outside, but Makayla's been through a lot all these years."

The life of an officer's spouse is no walk in the park. The long hours and unpredictable dangers of police work can strain even the strongest of relationships.

The comment about Makayla hit Adam hard. He could never quite convince himself that Ann's murder wasn't some-how related to his job. He was silent for some time until he finally said, "Marcus, you're my closest friend and the best damn detective I know. If this is something you and Makayla need to do, I'm all in."

"I appreciate that. I just had to get it off my chest. You need to know that it's something we're considering, but nothing's set in stone." Marcus smiled. "But either way, eat your muffin. We've got a long night ahead of us."

CHAPTER TWO

IT WAS QUIET for a Friday night in downtown Charleston. There were the normal traffic accidents, bar fights, and domestic incidents, but nothing requiring Adam and Marcus to leave the station until around 3:00 a.m.

Just after the hour, a 911 call came in from a woman who reported strange sounds and witnessed someone leaving her neighbor's house at the corner of Rutledge and Queen across from Colonial Lake Park. The woman identified her neighbor as Dr. Charles Richardson. Officers Bud Miller and Jay Rivers were dispatched and arrived at the address a few minutes later. They parked several houses from the subject's address, and after identifying the woman who made the 911 call and ordering her to remain inside, they approached Richardson's house. Noticing the front door was partially ajar, they drew their

Glock 19s—holding them in the two-handed low ready position.

After situating themselves on either side of the door, Miller knocked and loudly announced their presence. "Police officers! Identify yourself! Identify yourself!"

No response. Miller gave his partner a hand signal indicating he would enter first. Using his left hand, he carefully eased the door open so they could see inside. Rivers followed him in; arms extended in the front ready position. The house was quiet, but their eyes were immediately drawn to a figure stretched out beside a heavyset coffee table. Blood had spread around the body's chest, and a closer look revealed what appeared to be a single gunshot to the head.

Miller signaled he would clear the rest of the first floor. Even though it was clear the man was dead, Rivers bent down to check for a pulse. He found none. A short time later, Miller returned and confirmed the first floor was clear. Once it was established the second floor was also clear, they called headquarters. Not wanting to compromise the crime scene, the officers went outside, checked the perimeter of the house, and waited for the detectives and additional officers.

Two squad cars showed up, and officers were in the process of securing crime scene tape across the entrance when Adam and Marcus arrived. Most of the homes in the area were upscale. Even the tragic circumstances couldn't keep Adam's eyes from roving appreciatively over the well-appointed porticos. Most of the homes in the area had been built for wealthy residents a hundred years ago, and they were only sold when someone even wealthier came along. The house Richardson lived in was on the smaller side but still valued well in excess of $1 million.

Adam approached the officers. "What have we got?"

"We approached the door and noticed it was open," Miller started. "No response when we identified ourselves. Entered and found one adult male on the first floor. Deceased. Multiple gunshot wounds to the chest and a single shot to the head. Inside clear and perimeter secured. EMS and CSI have been notified and are en route."

"You said the door was open. Any evidence of a forced entry?"

"Sorry, sir. Didn't check."

"Where is the person who called it in?" Adam asked.

The officer pointed next door. "She's inside, sir. My partner is with her."

By now, lights were beginning to appear in several houses and curious residents were stepping onto their porches.

"We're going next door," Adam said. "Make sure you keep the area clear."

They entered the woman's house and introduced themselves. Her name was Emma Harris. She was small, not much more than five feet, and appeared to be in her mid-to-late-seventies. She was holding a small white dog.

"Ma'am," Marcus began, "please tell us what you heard and saw before you called 911."

"Well now, Sadie here gets me up most every night. Poor girl's getting old like me, and I have to take her out to pee, or she makes a mess. I don't mind getting up, though. At my age, I don't sleep very well anymore. Oh, dear, I remember when I could sleep like a baby. Anyway, I was outside, and Sadie was doing her business when I heard something next door."

"That would be Dr. Richardson's house?" Marcus asked.

"Yes. Charles is his first name. And he doesn't like anyone calling him Charlie. Oh my, I hope he's all right."

"Can you describe the sound you heard?"

"Well, it was a funny sound—kind of like a 'snap.' There were two 'snaps' and then another one a moment later. At first, I thought it might be that newspaper boy. He always throws the papers on our porches. But, Lord, it was the middle of the night. Well, Sadie, she scampers over to Charles' lawn and starts yippin' to beat the band. That's when I saw this man leave Charles' house. He looked at me, and I think I surprised him. Then he jogged around the other side of the house—Sadie still yippin' away. Can I get you something to drink? I can make some tea."

"No thank you, ma'am," Marcus said. "Will you please show us where you were when you heard those sounds and saw the person jogging around Dr. Richardson's house? You said it was a man, correct?"

"I think so. He had on one of those hooded sweatshirts—like it was about thirty degrees cooler than it is."

"I see."

Ms. Harris took Adam and Marcus outside and down her front steps onto a small lawn—positioning herself approximately five feet to the right of the bottom stair.

"Thank you, ma'am. Now, could you describe the man?"

"Oh, dear. It was so dark. I just don't know."

"Could you tell if the person was tall or short, black or white?"

"I'm sorry, officer. I remember he was pretty tall. He might have been white, but I only saw him for a second before he disappeared around the house."

"That helps," Marcus said. "I'd like you to close your eyes and see if you can remember anything else about him."

Harris closed her eyes and tried to visualize the man leaving Dr. Richardson's house. She scrunched her face for a few seconds, and then her eyes popped open.

"Now I remember! The man limped when he jogged around the house—like his leg was hurting him. That's when I called 911. The girl that answered was very nice. I was a little nervous, but she calmed me down."

"Do you remember if he favored his right or left leg?"

"Let me see." She closed her eyes again. "His right leg. Yes, it looked like his right leg hurt."

"Good. Now does Dr. Richardson live by himself?" Adam asked.

"Oh, yes. Sometimes he has lady friends over, but he lives by himself. He rents the house from Dr. White. The Whites live on Daniel Island. They're very nice people."

"Thank you, Ms. Harris," Marcus said. "Just one more thing. Do you happen to know if Dr. Richardson has any relatives in the area?"

"Let me see. I do remember he told me he had a brother that lived in Pittsburgh, but he never mentioned any family here in Charleston."

"Thank you, Ms. Harris," Marcus said. "You've been very helpful. The officer will stay with you, and someone will be by shortly to take your statement."

As Ms. Harris rescaled the stairs, Adam said, "Usually folks mistake gunfire like the pop of a firework, but the fact that she described it like the snap of a newspaper hitting the house makes me think there might be a suppressor involved. This was no casual robbery. Sounds like it could've been a professional hit. The officer said the victim was shot twice to the chest and once to the head. I figure the first two shots took him down, and the third was the kill shot."

"Possibly," Marcus replied. "But why target Richardson?"

Adam smiled and said, "That's why we're here, partner."

Adam and Marcus slipped on crime scene gloves and booties before entering Richardson's. One tech was taking pictures of the body, and two more were in the living room assessing the situation. They acknowledged the techs and while waiting for the photographer to finish, checked the front door.

"I don't see any evidence of forced entry," Adam said.

"Techs can confirm that," Marcus replied and scanned the living room. It was impressive. A large flat screen TV was mounted above a granite fireplace and oriental rugs covered the hand-scraped Brazilian cherry hardwood floor. The furniture had a masculine look to it and was definitely high-end. Adam had checked out the kitchen and was now in a small office to the right of the front door. Two leather chairs stood alongside a good-sized wooden desk that held an Apple iMac.

Careful not to step in the pool of blood—Marcus inspected the body which was lying on its right side. The dead man wore a pair of designer jeans and a blood-soaked polo pullover. Upon closer inspection, one bullet had struck him in the upper chest, another in the abdomen. The third bullet had entered the right frontal lobe directly above the eye socket—the kill shot. The man's eyes were closed.

"Looks like Richardson might have let the killer in," Marcus observed.

"Yeah, three o'clock in the morning, and the guy was still dressed."

Marcus bent down and pointed at the area around the man's face and chest. "What's that stuff?"

Adam took a closer look and said, "Don't know. Looks like dirt or sand."

"That doesn't make any sense," Marcus said, "This place is immaculate." He used his cell phone to take a picture of the material and told one of the crime scene techs to secure a sample.

Continuing their search upstairs, the detectives found three bedrooms and two baths. Like downstairs, the furniture in the master bedroom was impressive with several original paintings hung on the walls. The closet was filled with suitcoats, slacks, shirts, shoes, and a variety of other expensive clothing.

"Jesus, Marcus. That looks like a Hart Schaffner Marx store!"

There was another smaller bedroom and a third room with mirrored walls filled with workout equipment and weights. It all looked new and pricey.

They went back downstairs, left the house, and let the techs continue their work. As they were leaving, they spotted the blue and white coroner's van—Alice O'Sullivan and her assistant were approaching the house. Alice was the Charleston County deputy coroner and had been around as long as Adam could remember.

O'Sullivan was wearing a Carolina Panthers' ball cap, a baggy sweatshirt, and corduroys. "All right, Stone. This better be good. The damn call yanked me out of a dream just as George Clooney was knocking on my bedroom door!"

Adam smiled. "Sorry, Alice, but George is going to have to wait."

"Where's my customer?" she asked.

"The body's inside. The techs are still working the scene. Go on in and do what you do. We'll be around. Just let us know what you think when you're done."

As Alice went inside, one of Charleston's K-9 units pulled up and a couple familiar faces popped out—Larry Miles and his German shepherd, Strider. Adam and Marcus had worked with Larry on several Special Operations drug task force investigations.

"Good morning, detectives," Miles said.

"How've you been, Larry?" Adam asked.

"Can't complain. Understand you've got a 10-105. With the uptick in downtown drug activity lately, Lockwood wants

K-9 involved in any possible homicide. What have you got for me?"

Adam told Miles that O'Sullivan and CSI were still working inside the house and explained what they'd learned so far about the murder. Fifteen minutes later, O'Sullivan exited the house, trailed by her assistant wheeling the bagged corpse on a gurney.

"The tech guys couldn't find any shell casings," O'Sullivan said, "so it looks like a revolver. Based on the entry wounds, I say maybe a Ruger or a small S&W. The victim was shot three times, but CSI only recovered one slug. It looks like a .22LR caliber. Ballistics can confirm that. I anticipate finding the other two bullets in the body, but I can verify that when I do the autopsy."

"When do you think you'll get started?" Marcus asked.

"I need to sleep a little more, but I'll get on it as soon as I get up. I should have some preliminaries later today. Good luck on your investigation, boys. I'm out of here. George is waiting for me."

Adam checked with the techs, returned a moment later, and gave the go ahead for Strider to do his thing.

Inside, the police dog was all business as he systematically moved through the living room searching for the familiar scent of drugs.

Adam was endlessly amazed at what these dogs could do. Narcotic detection dogs, or "sniffers," are trained to recognize seven basic odors, allowing them to detect narcotics of different types and compositions. He'd heard that some scientists believe their sense of smell is tens of thousands of times more sensitive than humans'. And the unique anatomy of their nose detects odors at concentrations somewhere between 10 and 500 parts per trillion.

Strider moved to the second floor and was working the master bedroom when he suddenly stopped and sat directly in front of a closet. Miles moved the hanging clothes aside exposing a flat wooden panel painted the same color as the sheetrock. The panel was approximately 3' by 4' and held against the back wall by four corner screws. Marcus used his multipurpose pocketknife to remove the panel, revealing a heavy-duty electronic safe bolted flush to the wall.

"Good boy, Strider!" Miles praised his dog. "That's my good boy!" He turned toward the detectives. "I think we just hit paydirt. Definitely drugs inside there. And that's one of those high-tech fingerprint safes."

Marcus took pictures of the wooden panel and safe while Adam called headquarters requesting a locksmith.

When Marcus finished taking pictures, he retrieved the keys to Richardson's BMW so Miles and Strider could check out the car. The dog sniffed around the exterior, interior, and the trunk—no drugs. The BMW would be transferred to the forensic garage where it would be disassembled and thoroughly searched.

After Miles left, Adam told Marcus that their locksmith would be there in about a half-hour. "Come on, buddy, let's take another look inside."

They entered the house and went directly into the office just to the right of the entrance. CSI had taken Richardson's computer so the techs at Lockwood could analyze its contents.

"Listen, partner," Marcus started, "if someone did take out Richardson, why would a doctor warrant a professional hit? Drugs or gambling debts is what usually does it. Keep your eyes peeled for anything out of the ordinary."

Adam opened the center desk drawer and found a box of Richardson's business cards—Dr. Charles Richardson, president of PRO Care Sports Medicine in North Charleston. Other assorted business cards were held together by a rubber band. Adam took a look, but nothing jumped out. Still, they would need to follow up on those contacts. Richardson's checkbook was also in the center drawer. He didn't expect to find anything shady in Richardson's personal checkbook but flipped through it anyway. The balance was maintained at around $5,000, and nothing looked overly suspicious.

Several file folders were in one of the larger side drawers. The folders contained receipts, car and health insurance agreements, several other documents—none that seemed out of the ordinary. Another drawer contained several brochures and catalogs for physical therapy products and equipment.

The desk had a glass top with four business cards slid underneath. One was for a Susan Novak, administrative assistant at PRO Care. The others belonged to three physicians in Greater Charleston—Samuel Morgan, Nathan Bell, and Ronald Jefferson. Adam took pictures with his cell phone and copied the names and phone numbers in his notepad.

"Marcus, take a look at these."

Marcus studied the cards and noted that all three doctors specialized in pain management. "It would make sense for a sports doctor like Richardson to refer patients to a pain specialist."

"I hear you," Adam answered. "The rent here has to be at least $5,000 a month. He drives a new $80,000 BMW 741i, and look at the way his place is furnished. The oriental rugs and art must cost more than I make in a year. I know doctors make a pretty penny, but I can't believe it's anywhere near enough to pay for this lifestyle."

"Right," Marcus replied. "And did you see the suits in his closet? I wouldn't be surprised if they cost a few thousand apiece. Maybe mommy and daddy left him an inheritance. Maybe he's just living beyond his means. Looks like there's drugs in that safe, but the question is—what kind and how much? Maybe I'm wrong, but this whole scene smells like a drug hit."

~~~~

Twenty-five minutes later the Lowcountry Lock & Safe van pulled up, and a tall, thin man exited with a large case. His face was a mass of freckles, and his hair was bright red and tied in a ponytail.

"Hello, detectives. Name's Burt Willis. I got the call from Lockwood."
~~~~

Adam and Marcus introduced themselves, and on the way into the house, Marcus explained the police dog's discovery in the upstairs bedroom closet. "I don't know anything about safes, but this one looks pretty heavy-duty."

In the master bedroom, Willis set his case aside, and all 6', 7" of him bent into a catcher's crouch to study the safe. "That's a Barska Biometric. Accessed with the owner's fingerprint. I'll have to drill this one."

"Do whatever you need to do," Adam said.

"All right. Should take about thirty to forty minutes."

Willis had Adam sign a waiver and then opened his case and removed a templet containing two sets of square openings on either side of a center point. He placed the center point over the spot where he would drill out the locking mechanism and marked each of the four corner holes. After drilling the holes, he removed a piece of bracketed metal he used to center the drill in the precise location. Once centered, it was attached to the safe with self-setting bolts. The electric power drill with a long titanium bit was secured to the bracket. He put on gloves and safety goggles and began drilling. It was an exceedingly slow process with Willis constantly adjusting the drill and cooling the bit.

Adam decided to stay and watch the procedure while Marcus left to get an update from the crime scene techs and check with the officers who were canvassing the area. The neighborhood was alive with activity as more police officers had arrived and were going door to door questioning the residents.

Marcus returned just as the drilling was completed. Willis removed his goggles and opened the door to the safe.

"Well, I'll be damned," Marcus muttered. He took out his cell phone and took a picture of the contents.

The upper portion of the safe was filled with large plastic bottles—each containing oxycodone pills. Adam put on crime scene gloves and removed a bottle containing two thousand 30 mg pills. The label read *oxicodona*—the Spanish spelling of oxycodone. There were also several rubber-banded stacks of $50 and $100 bills. The lower section of the safe held three passports, a flash drive, six burner phones, and a key—*#128* on its chain.

He removed the key. "I wonder what this is to?"

"Maybe some sort of locker," Marcus answered. "Like you see at airports and bus terminals. It's numbered, so it's probably somewhere that has a bunch of lockers or locks. Heck, could be to almost anything."

Adam interrupted Marcus—telling Willis to keep what he'd seen to himself.

"Hey, guys," he answered, "my lips are sealed. Your department is one of my biggest customers. No way am I going to mess that up."

"Good," Marcus said. "You did a good job, Willis. Now, get yourself packed up and out of here."

"Yes, sir!"

As soon as Willis left, Adam removed a stack of bills and pointed to the safe. "Looks like our Dr. Richardson was dealing a different kind of therapy on the side."

Marcus shook his head and said, "There must be forty to fifty thousand pills in there, and I'll bet you a six-pack those pain doctors are in on this. If Richardson's dealing this much OXY, there's no way he's not connected to organized crime— the cartel, mafia, one of the local gangs."

Adam's lips set in a grim line. "Respectable" doctors like this had bedeviled the task force for years. Since it's up to them to self-report, many of them end up running their own pill mills, like street pushers with much better lawyers.

"These asshole doctors are no better than street pushers," Adam muttered.

"Agreed," Marcus offered. "Now we need to get the techs up here to bag and tag all this. We can't afford to have some lawyer say we 'pulled an O.J.' on this one." The phrase obviously referring to the O.J. Simpson case.

~~~~

Slowly the soft grays of dawn gave way to morning's light, and the Holy City was once again waking up to a new day.

Adam told the patrol officers to stay at the scene until forensics finished up and to make sure the house was locked up and the front door taped.

The detectives were driving back to the station when Adam said, "Listen, I figure the computer guys won't have anything for us off Richardson's computer and cell phone until early this afternoon. When we get back, I'll get the murder book started and follow up on Richardson's brother and the
~~~~

people who rented him the house. You can catch a few hours of sleep, and I'll get some shuteye when you get up. We're going to be on this 24/7 and need to grab sleep whenever we can."

"Works for me," Marcus answered. "This is when Makayla reminds me the kind of hours I could keep if I were working for her dad."

"I'm sure there's a key for Richardson's office among the evidence the techs recovered from his house. If we can get Judge Roberts to sign off on a warrant by late afternoon, we can check out Richardson's office this evening."

"We also need to bring Boyer up to speed on what we have. I'm sure he knows about the murder by now. We can also ask him to check with our undercover street people to see what they know about the distribution of opioids around here. Wasn't too long ago Max DiMarco was running a scheme to steal narcotics from Mercy Hospital."

"That was three or four years ago now—hard to believe," Adam recalled. "We know the Posse, the Bloods, and the cartel were never that interested in pills. It's my guess that if Richardson is connected, it's going to be with Nick Santoro."

"All that may be true but don't forget Santoro is a prime suspect in Joe Wallace's and Tanya Scarcella's murders."

Adam shook his head. "Nick Santoro is always a suspect in something, and it's never stopped him from doing the mob's business."

CHAPTER THREE

ADAM HAD MADE a few phone calls and was getting the murder book started when his desk phone rang.

"Stone, I need you in my office, now!"

It was Frank Boyer. A minute later, Adam was pushing into Boyer's office.

"Sit down, Stone. Tell me about this shooting."

Adam gave Boyer the short version—not going too deep into the amount of money and drugs found in the safe. Boyer had the reputation of cutting people off if they went into too much detail. He'd often describe himself as a "big picture" guy.

"Where's Williams?" he asked.

"In the Bunkhouse catching a few hours."

"What the hell is he doing there? He should be working this."

It was Boyer's first murder case, and he clearly wasn't interested in having it drag out.

"Frank, we're on it." Adam was trying hard to keep his cool. "We're doing what we can with what we have so far. Forensics and O'Sullivan won't have anything for us until later this afternoon. I'm getting the murder book started and running down any next of kin for Richardson."

"All right, then get to it."

Adam remained seated and said, "You could do us a favor, though. Marcus and I've spent most of our time on the heroin and cocaine side. It would be helpful if you could have one of your undercovers give us some background on who's controlling the opioid pill market and how they're moving product."

"You can do that yourself, Stone. Just make sure you let me know what's happening on Richardson. Chief Merchant is expecting an update from me."

Adam was leaving the office thinking just how difficult it was going to be with Boyer running the show.

He had been back at his desk for a while when he heard someone say, "Detective Stone, I've got something for you."

Adam looked up and recognized one of the computer techs he'd worked with several months ago on the Joe Wallace murder case. His first name was Steve. Last name? Adam was drawing a blank.

"Hey, Steve. What you got?"

"Yes, sir. I've been working on that computer from the crime scene. Most of what I've found so far seems pretty normal for someone's personal computer." Steve handed Adam a manila folder. "These are copies of Dr. Richardson's calendar and contact list. I've made a quick review of his photos, emails, letters, and Excel files. There's obviously a lot more to check out, but, like I said, I haven't come across anything that raised a major red flag."

"What about the flash drive?"

"I was just getting to that, sir. I only got it about a half-hour ago. All I've seen so far is a bunch of spreadsheets. It's kind of hard to follow because most of the headings and categories are labeled in some sort of code. But it's clear the spreadsheets contain records of the number and dollar amounts of something. I'll continue to work on it, but I made you a copy of the flash drive. I thought you and Detective Williams might be able to figure it out."

Adam took the flash drive and said, "I have an idea that whatever's in here probably has something to do with drugs—pills to be specific. So, make sure that's your mindset as you continue. That flash drive could hold clues to who killed that doctor."

"I hear you." Steve was about to leave, but stopped and said, "I just wanted to say it's good to be working with you and Detective Williams again."

Adam smiled. "Thanks, Steve. Same here."

Adam took a deep breath and realized it was time to call Richardson's brother. His mind quickly scanned for tasks to delay, but he just had to suck it up. These calls were definitely one of the most difficult parts of being a cop, and the responsibility almost always rested with the detectives working the case. He dialed the cell number, and it was answered after the first ring.

"Hello."

"Is this Randell Richardson?"

"Yes. Who's calling?"

"Mr. Richardson, I'm Detective Stone calling from the Police Department in Charleston, South Carolina. This is about your brother."

"What about him?"

"I'm sorry, but I need to inform you that your brother was found dead early this morning in his house." The line was quiet for several seconds. "Mr. Richardson?"

"I'm here. How did it happen?" The voice was surprisingly calm.

"Our officers responded to a 911 call last night from one of his neighbors. When they arrived at his house, they found that he'd been shot. We're very sorry for your loss. Are there family members in the Charleston area? We will need his next of kin to identify the body and make the necessary burial and probate arrangements."

"No, our parents passed away quite some time ago. There's just the two of us, and to be honest, Charles and I haven't spoken in years. But I understand what needs to be done. I'll make arrangements to be there in the next day or two."

"Thank you, sir."

Adam turned his attention to his computer and was just about to insert the flash drive when he was interrupted by a call from Dr. Sam White, Richardson's landlord.

"Thank you for the call, doctor. I understand Charles Richardson leased your house on Rutledge."

"Yes, sir, he does. Is there a problem?"

"I'm afraid there is, sir. I'm sorry, but Dr. Richardson was found dead this morning in the home."

"Dear Lord," White gasped. "What happened?"

"We're working on finding that out. But I can tell you that Dr. Richardson was shot. I realize this is a shock, but I do have some questions I need to ask."

"Certainly. Go right ahead."

"Thank you, sir. How long did Dr. Richardson live at the Rutledge location?"

"Let me see. I would say he's been there four or five years now. To be honest, we didn't know him that well, but he was a good tenant, and as far as I know, a good enough doctor."

"I see," Adam said. "Did the master bedroom have a safe installed in the closet?"

"Excuse me?"

"The closet in the upstairs bedroom," Adam repeated. "Was there a safe installed there?"

"A safe? No, there were no safes in the house at all."

"I see, sir. There was no damage to the house, but we will need to keep it secure for a while. We will advise you when you're able to access the premises."

"I understand."

~~~~

It was approaching noon, and Adam was about to go wake up Marcus when he saw him entering the bullpen.

"So," Marcus said, "did you come up with anything good?"

"I've been busy while you were snoozing away," Adam said, as he brought his partner up to speed.

"Interesting," Marcus said. "Anything else?"

"Yeah, I talked to Boyer. He wanted to make sure we hurry up and solve *his* murder case. I asked him to contact his undercover detectives for opioid intel, and he told us to do it ourselves. Apparently, he's too busy organizing things. What an asswipe."

"Yeah," Marcus agreed, "I figure he was always pissed that we were part of Merchant's Special Operations Unit and reported directly to Ed."

"The guy's definitely insecure," Adam said. "Anyway, remember Steve, the computer tech that helped in the Wallace murder?"

"Sure. Steve Gagyi. Nice guy." "

"He was working on the flash drive we found in the safe and said it was filled with spreadsheets." Adam held up the drive he got from Steve. "He made us a copy. Let's take a look."

"Sounds like I woke up just in time. Glad I grabbed some coffee."
~~~~

Adam opened the flash drive and found a list of twenty-some Excel files. He opened the first, entitled **Asclepius.** It had thirteen columns, one per month and one for the totals. The first nine months had been filled in. Each month was divided into a "**#**" and a "**$**" column. The spreadsheet was broken into three sections—**M, B,** and **J**.

"Perhaps the Drs. Morgan, Bell, and Jefferson," Adam added pointing at the three capital letters.

Three rows were under each section: **O-20, O-30,** and **O-40**.

Adam and Marcus studied the spreadsheet for a moment.

"All right," Marcus said. "It's obvious the three O's refer to the oxycodone dosages—20, 30, and 40 mgs. It's also obvious the # and $ symbols are the pills totals and their cost. But what's an **Asclepius**?"

"Hang on," Adam said and googled it. "Ah, it's the Greek god of medicine."

"Heck, Adam! That spreadsheet shows the number and dollar amount of the pills those doctors sold each month."

"Yeah," Adam replied, "it could mean what the doctors sold or what Richardson sold to the doctors. Either way, that's a hell of a lot of pills. Look at those totals. Those doctors are averaging over $500,000 a month of that shit!"

The next twenty sheets had the same basic layout of data, but they appeared to track data for only one person. The individuals were identified only with their last name.

"These people are probably direct clients of Richardson," Adam said. "And it looks like he's pulling in another forty or fifty-grand from them every month."

Richardson had deleted the data on five of the spread-sheets but for some reason did not delete the names. Marcus pointed at the screen.

"I bet those five names are clients Richardson no longer sells to. The date next to each name is probably when he quit supplying them."

Adam agreed, took screen shots with his cell, and copied down the last names of the twenty individuals.

There were a few more spreadsheets in the file—each had a series of calculations generating a total dollar amount. It wasn't immediately clear what they referred to, but judging by the dollar amounts, a hell of a lot of money was involved!

Adam was removing the UBS drive when Marcus said, "This is all good intel, but we still don't know where Richardson was getting his OXY—and more importantly who murdered him."

CHAPTER FOUR

BY THE TIME Adam and Marcus had finished taking their first crack at analyzing the flash drive info, it was a shade after 3:00 Saturday afternoon—12 hours after the murder. Adam was jacked and refused to sleep, so they decided to check in with Steve to see what he'd come up with.

Marcus explained what they'd learned from the spreadsheets.

"That's what I figured, too," Steve said. "I took those twenty names and checked them against Richardson's contact list on both his computer and his cell phone. I struck out on both counts."

"Don't worry about that," Adam said. "There's a chance we might find them when we check out his office. To be honest, I doubt Richardson called these people on his personal cell. He probably met them in person or used a burner like we found in his safe. Just keep working on his computer and cell phone and keep us posted."

"You can do something for us, though," Marcus added. "Remember those initials on the first spreadsheet—M, B, and J. We're pretty sure the initials are for the doctors Richardson was supplying OXY to." Marcus had written down the names and handed the paper to Steve. "Do your magic and see what you can find on them."

"No problem," Steve replied. "Give me an hour or so."

~~~~

When they returned to their desks, Adam had a message that Judge Roberts had approved the warrant request for Richardson's office, and it was ready to be picked up at the courthouse.

"I'll go grab that," Adam said. "Why don't you go ahead and see if Alice has anything on the autopsy?"

"That works. Listen, I can't stomach anything else from the vending machine. When you get back, let's grab something to eat on our way to Richardson's office."

Adam left, and Marcus called O'Sullivan's office at the county morgue. She was in the lab and Marcus got rerouted to her.

A moment later, Alice answered, "Marcus, I'm glad you called. I'm in the middle of working on our boy right now."

"Anything you can tell me yet?"
~~~~

"Not too much, but here's what I've got. No defensive wounds on the victim's hands or arms, however I did find a contusion above the left ear. There was only one exit wound, and I found the two .22's inside the body like I thought I would. The shot to the abdomen was the through and through. The chest shot lodged in the right ventricle, and the headshot bounced around his brain. It looked like scrambled eggs in there. I did a clinical screen, and Richardson had a BAC of .17. And you know what that means—the dude was totally blitzed—must have been drinking all night. I found no other drugs in his system, but the full tox screen won't be back until tomorrow.

"There was something strange when CSI pulled a sample of Richardson's blood from his shirt. There were small grains of material embedded in the blood. A mass spectrometry run on the material identified it as find silica sand."

"Any idea where it came from?" Marcus asked.

"Not a clue. I checked his internal organs, and they all looked good. I'd say other than being dead, Richardson was a pretty healthy guy."

"Thanks, Alice. Let us know when your final report is ready, and we'll send someone over to pick it up."

"You got it."

Marcus was about to hang up but stopped and said, "Oh, and just curious—was Clooney still in your bedroom when you got back?"

"You bet your ass he was!"

~~~~

Adam got ahold of Richardson's assistant, Susan Novak. At first, she refused to accept the fact that Richardson was dead. She thought it was someone making a sick joke, but after Adam described the circumstances surrounding his death, she broke down. Once Adam was able to calm her, she agreed to meet him at Richardson's office at 7:00 that evening.

Adam hung up, and Marcus asked how she took the news.

"As well as to be expected when someone gets a call like that."

"I say we send an officer to sit on Richardson's office until we get there. We don't want Novak getting into his office before we get there."

"Good idea," Adam said. "If she is part of Richardson's scheme, we don't want her messing with any evidence."

~~~~

They left for Richardson's PRO Care office and stopped on the way to grab something to eat at Checkers on Remount. They ordered and found a table in the back.

"All right," Marcus said. "Let's back up and talk about what we've got so far and what we need to find out."

"Good," Adam agreed. "I'll start. We know the murder occurred at approximately 3:00 a.m. Saturday. Neighbor reported seeing a tall man with a limp leaving Richardson's house shortly after three shots were fired. No casings indicates a revolver was the murder weapon. Sounds like a suppressor was used. Two shots to the body, one to the head. Body was found just inside the living room. He was fully clothed at three o'clock in the morning. There's a chance he knew the killer."

"Right," Marcus interrupted. "The techs found no evidence of forced entry. Maybe the killer was a damn good lock artist. Alice told me she couldn't find any defensive wounds, but he did have a contusion on the side of his head. According to his BAC, Richardson was really smashed and probably had no clue what was going on. Assuming this was a hit, I can see how the killer might have waited for Richardson to come home. Richardson disarms the security system, and the killer whacks him on the head and puts three bullets into him. He hears Ms. Harris' dog barking and takes off."

"That makes sense," Adam said. "You got to figure this was a drug murder. Richardson was using his medical practice as a front for distributing opioids. If the numbers on those spreadsheets are even close to correct, there's no way Richardson could be doing this thing by himself. He's got to be connected. And it's my guess he was working with Nick Santoro. Seems like half the cases we deal with end up leading back to the operation run by Santoro, doesn't it?"

"Right," agreed Marcus, "and it looks like we've got our first suspect—Nick Santoro. Hopefully, we'll learn more from Richardson's office. At this point, I doubt we have enough to get warrants to search the offices of those three doctors."

They were finishing their meals when Marcus brought out the folder Steve had prepared on the three doctors Richardson was supplying.

"Samuel Morgan's divorced and lives in the Harborwalk townhouses on James Island," Marcus began. "His practice is on Folly Road. Bell's also divorced—condo and office in Mt. Pleasant. Dr. Jefferson is the only one with a family—he lives and practices on Daniel Island. All their practices are small like Richardson's—just themselves and an assistant. Steve did a heck of a job putting this together. I made a copy for you. There's a bunch more background on all three in here. For example, get this—Dr. Samuel Morgan was put on probation by the State Board ten years ago for the inappropriate prescribing of opioids."

Adam scanned the information in the folder and said, "The kid's really good." He checked his watch. "I'll read this later. We need to roll."

Five minutes later they were waiting outside the PRO Care office. It was in a small strip mall with five units facing Remount Road. PRO Care was on the far right, with an accounting business next door. Carolina Payday Loans, a nail salon, and a vacancy rounded out the units.

"Not exactly where you'd expect to find a hotshot doctor's office," Adam said.

Ten minutes passed before a late model white Mercedes-Benz GLC 350 pulled up next to Adam's Charger. Susan Novak got out carrying her handbag. She was about five-foot-seven with long blond hair. Her makeup was flawless, and the loose-fitting black chiffon pants and white silk blouse seemed a bit overdone for the occasion. To say she was attractive would have been an understatement. As she approached the detectives, they saw that her eyes were red—she'd been crying.

Adam showed his shield and introduced Marcus. "Thank you for coming, Ms. Novak. I realize this must be a shock to you." Adam took out the search warrant and showed it to her. "This warrant gives us legal authority to enter and search the office. We need you to open the door and disarm the security system."

"All right, give me a minute here." She rummaged through her purse, pulled out a set of keys, and opened the office door. She turned on the fluorescent lights and punched the code into the security panel. "Please tell me what happen to Charles. I can't believe he's dead."

Marcus gave her the basic details, not mentioning a thing about the drugs. "Please have a seat, Ms. Novak. I want to thank you again for helping us out. Detective Stone and I will take a quick look around, and then we'll have some questions for you."

Two leather chairs, a copier, two large filing cabinets, and Ms. Novak's desk filled the cramped reception area. There was a small storage closet and restroom in the back. Requisite marsh and seascape prints were hung without much care.

A door led to a large room with two waist-high cushioned tables, a treadmill, an elliptical, rubber mats, and a variety of other exercise equipment. Framed posters showing various stretching exercises hung on three of the walls along with a few motivational posters. One read; *Success is the Best Revenge!* Another read; *Results or Excuses—But not Both!* And large block letters were painted on the far wall:

PRO Care Sports Medicine
Step Away from Pain!

Marcus glanced at Adam who rolled his eyes in reaction to the sign on the wall. Richardson's personal office held a leather couch and chairs and a large glass-topped desk. Detailed sketches showing the human muscle and bone structure hung on the walls along with the doctor's degrees and certificates. There were several oil paintings of seascapes on the walls, and an Apple iMac desktop similar to the one in his home office sat on the desk. It was obvious that money wasn't a concern in furnishing both his home and his personal office.

Adam had been taking pictures and decided to question Novak before conducting a more thorough search. He went back to the reception area and asked Susan to open her computer. "I'm assuming you have a list of clients on there."

"Yes, of course."

"Can you filter them by current and former?"

"Sure. Give me a second." Novak booted up her computer and opened the client list. She applied the filter, and a second later the two lists appeared on her monitor. There looked to be approximately 75 current clients and several hundred former ones.

Adam opened his notepad and asked Novak if any of the twenty names he had copied from the spreadsheets were clients. She searched and only found matches for two: Kyle Perry and Sylvia Porter, both former clients. And according to their interpretation of the spreadsheets, Richardson had also stopped supplying them. The date after Perry's name was 7/6/2016, and the one behind Porter's was 11/20/2019.

"I'll need contact information for both of them," Adam said.

"I'm not sure I can do that. You know, patient confidentiality rules."

Adam held up the search warrant. "I'm not asking for medical records, Ms. Novak. Just addresses and phone numbers."

"Okay, I guess I can do that." She printed the information for the two former patients.

Adam asked if she recognized any of the fifteen names he believed to be Richardson's direct clients. She hesitated, but then said, "No. None of them were patients."

"How long have you worked at PRO Care, and what do you do here?"

"Gee, it's been a little over two years now. I file insurance paperwork, take care of billing, and pretty much everything else except see patients."

"I see," Adam said. He checked his notepad. "We know PRO Care has a continuing relationship with Drs. Samuel Morgan, Nathan Bell, and Ronald Jefferson. Correct?"

"Yes, but we work with a lot of doctors."

"I see. Do you refer many patients to pain management specialists?"

"Charles doesn't often do that, but sometimes it's a necessary part of a patient's overall rehabilitation program. Charles is always talking about the terrible opioid epidemic in our country and only refers patients as a last resort."

It was Adam's turn to look at Marcus who raised his eyebrows at that last comment.

"Ms. Novak," Marcus began, "is there a way you could tell us how many patients Dr. Richardson has referred to the three doctors Detective Stone mentioned?"

"I don't have that information on my computer, but Charles could probably give you an idea." She frowned and looked as if she was going to cry again. "Oh dear, here I am talking like Charles is still alive."

Adam handed her a tissue from the box on her desk.

"Detective Williams and I are going to be in Dr. Richardson's office for a while. If you have a spare flash drive, please go ahead and make a copy of those client lists for us."

"I can do that."

They entered the office and went directly to Richardson's desk. Adam would arrange to have the iMac picked up and analyzed, so they didn't mess with that. They started by methodically inspecting the desk drawers, keeping their eyes out for hidden compartments as they went. Adam poked around the office while Marcus left to do a more thorough inspection of the storage closet, bathroom, and main therapy room. He returned about fifteen minutes later.

"Any luck?" questioned Adam.

"I did find two pill bottles like we saw in Richardson's safe and a few boxes of pill vials," Adam said. "We'll have to wait to see what the techs come up with. Let's get back to Ms. Novak."

"Thanks for your patience, Ms. Novak," Adam said. "We're almost done here. Our computer technicians will be by later tonight to collect your computers. We have a key, but we'll need the security code."

"I suppose I can do that, but what am I going to do Monday morning? We have patients coming."

"I understand. I suggest telling them Dr. Richardson had an emergency, and you will let them know about rescheduling."

"What's going to happen to me? I mean without Charles, there's no business."

"I don't know," Adam said. "I hope you can figure something out." He gave her his business card and told her they would be in contact.

They waited until Novak left before getting into their car. "Well, what do you think about our Ms. Novak?" Marcus asked.

"She seemed genuinely upset about his death," Adam answered. "The question is whether she was pushing OXY with Richardson."

"Honestly, I can't see how she couldn't be involved. There were just the two of them in the office, and you saw that car she drove. You don't see many single secretaries at small companies driving a $60,000 Mercedes 350. And tell me that wasn't a Prada handbag she was toting."

"I agree," Adam said. "Let's get the forensic techs out here tonight. We don't want her messing around with those computers. Maybe they have a clue about who killed Richardson, but so far this has been a bust."

CHAPTER FIVE

THEY HAD JUST left Richardson's office, and Marcus noticed Adam was struggling to stay awake. He hadn't slept in over forty-eight hours. "Listen, partner, drop me off at the station and go on home for a few hours. I feel fine, and I've got plenty to do to keep me busy until you get back."

"Are you sure?"

"Go home, brother. You're fading. Sleep a few hours and get your ass back here. It's all good."

Adam dropped off Marcus, and it was approaching 10:00 p.m. by the time he made it back to his apartment. As he walked through the door, Tracy said, "Oh my Lord, Adam, you look terrible."

"Yeah, well it comes with the territory. Where's Piper?"

"She's spending the night at Chloe's. Sorry, dear, but I thought you'd be at the station all night."

"That's all right. I just need a few hours of sleep. Then I need to get back."

"You go on and get some sleep, dear. I'll have sandwiches in the fridge for when you leave."

Adam headed for his bedroom thinking how lucky he and Piper were to have Tracy part of their life. Lying in bed, his thoughts focused on his daughter. Despite the loving support Tracy gave Piper, Ann's death left an emotional void. Marcus' possible retirement made him think more about how much of Piper's life he was missing. He fell asleep weighing the sacrifices that had come with the career he had chosen. His alarm jolted him awake at 2:00 a.m. He took a quick shower, put on clean clothes, and grabbed the sandwiches Tracy had made. He was still tired when he arrived at the station, but after twenty years on the force, that was nothing new to him.

~~~~

Adam rounded the corner of the bullpen and saw someone in his chair across from Marcus. He got closer, saw the ponytail, and realized it was Terry Blackwood. He was in his normal street attire—old jeans, loose-fitting Hawaiian shirt, thick leather necklace. His thin face had about a week's worth of beard.

Blackwood had worked undercover vice for the past five years—the last year focused on opioids and hallucinogens.

Adam shook his hand and said, "Blackwood, you're looking spiffy. It's been a while. How've you been?"
~~~~

He responded with his normal, "Livin' the dream, my friend."

"I was telling Terry about the Richardson case," Marcus said.

Adam pulled up a chair. "We're hoping you could give us some intel on who's distributing pills around here and how they're doing it."

"Hell, yes, brother." Blackwood responded. "That's been my world for the past year or so. There're several pill players in Charleston, but most of them are small time. The big boy in town is Nick Santoro, and his people are in the process of eliminating the competition."

"Eliminating as in?" Adam asked.

Blackwood smiled. "By making them an offer they can't refuse. Most of the small timers are in no position to fuck with Santoro. And those that do sometimes disappear."

"Like Richardson?" Adam asked.

"Possibly," agreed Blackwood. "Sounds like your boy, Richardson, was moving a heck of a lot of product."

Marcus nodded. "We figured he was getting his supply from Nick Santoro, and Nick was getting it from his uncle, Eddie Santoro. We're pretty sure about the Chicago connection."

"You're right," Blackwood replied. "And the word is Chicago's bringing in opioids from China and distributing them to major cities throughout the Midwest and South."

"Shit," Adam said. "If that's the case, Richardson might have screwed up big time. The labels on his bottles of OXY were printed in Spanish. He must have been getting his product from Mexico, and I wouldn't be surprised if Nick Santoro had him killed to send a message to anyone else thinking about pushing the Mexican product."

"We're seeing Santoro make a big push into the schools in the suburbs," Blackwood said. "Hell, you know how expensive OXY is, and Charleston suburbs are fertile ground. We're seeing more and more kids getting addicted and eventually turning to cheap heroin to satisfy their habit."

Blackwood finally took off, and Adam and Marcus promised they'd keep him in the loop as the case progressed.

~~~~

After Blackwood left, the detectives talked about how to proceed with the investigation. They decided the next move would be to interview Kyle Perry and Sylvia Porter—Richardson's former patients turned direct clients. Then they'd interview the trio of doctors to whom Richardson referred patients.

At 7:00 Sunday morning, a weary Adam was heading to his desk when Boyer called out, "Hey, Stone, did you hear what happened last night out in Mt. Pleasant?"

"No, what?"

"Someone reported a break in around midnight at a condo out there. Cops got there and found the homeowner murdered inside."

"That's too bad, man," Adam said and started to walk away.
~~~~

"Hold on, Stone. The guy that was murdered was one of those pill doctors Richardson was supplying. Nathan Bell."

"Holy shit!"

"I thought you might be interested," Boyer smirked. "I suggest you and Williams get your asses out there, and you'd better call ahead and explain why you're coming. And don't take any shit from our friends across the river."

Twenty minutes later, Adam and Marcus arrived at 1523 Cambridge Lakes Drive. Five Mt. Pleasant cruisers were out front, and several officers were milling around a first-floor unit. Adam lifted the crime scene tape and introduced himself and Marcus to the attending officer.

The officer pointed to a group and said, "Detective Wrigley is over there. You'll need to speak to him."

"Thanks."

"Detective Wrigley," Adam said as the approached the group. A large man in a sport coat and tie open at the neck turned and said, "That would be me. Stone and Williams?"

They nodded and Wrigley directed one of the officers to give them crime scene gloves and booties. "Forensics is still working the scene. Come on, and I'll show you what we've got."

Bell's three-bedroom, two-bath condo was on the first floor. Wrigley led them through the living room into the master bedroom—the gleaming appliances and shining hardwood floors looked like they could have been installed yesterday. Nathan Bell's eyes were closed, and his body was lying flat on his king-sized bed—his arms crossed over his chest. The sheets and covers were bathed in blood which had pooled and congealed onto the otherwise immaculate hardwood floors. A chair was pulled up next the bed as if the killer had sat there for some time admiring his handiwork.

"Multiple gunshots to the body and one to the head," Detective Wrigley said. "Killed in his sleep."

"It looks like the body was staged," Adam suggested. "I mean look at the way he's lying—like he's in a casket."

Wrigley chuckled. "Yeah, I guess if you can get past the blood and the hole in his head, he looks like he's having a little nap. But this fella ain't waking up."

"Have the techs recovered casings or bullets?" Marcus asked.

"No casings, but we've got two .22 caliber bullets. Let's get out of here and let forensics finish their work. We can talk more outside."

As soon as they were out of the condo, Wrigley pulled out a cigarette and after lighting up, offered one to Adam and Marcus. They declined. He shook his head and said, "Gotta quit these things. Anyway, we heard about the murder of your Dr. Richardson Friday night and figured Bell might be connected in some way. Looks like our departments are joined at the hip on this one."

It was agreed that the forensic findings and the autopsy results would be exchanged, and the two departments would work together on the murders. Emails and phone numbers were exchanged.

Adam and Marcus were about to leave when Wrigley said, "One more thing, detectives. Let's agree not to have a pissing contest about who's running the show. You work your investigation and we'll work ours. But we both share what we find. No egos on this one. Agreed?"

"Wouldn't have it any other way, detective," Adam said. "We may have two dead bodies in two cities, but one son of a bitch probably killed both of them."

~~~~

They were back at the station and walking past Boyer's office.

"Williams and Stone, come in here a second."

They knew what was coming and Marcus mumbled, "Oh, shit. Here we go."

They entered and before Boyer could say another word, Adam said, "It's what it looks like, Captain. Both cases are related, and we're most likely dealing with one killer. Detective Wrigley agrees we need to work together on both cases."

"Yeah, well, I know Wrigley, and I'm not taking a back seat to Mt. Pleasant on this one. Any breaks on our case; you come to me first. Is that understood?"

"Sure, Captain," Adam said. "There's something else." Boyer glanced at his watch while Adam continued, "You know we're pretty sure Richardson was in bed with those three other doctors: Samuel Morgan, Nathan Bell, and Ronald Jefferson. Richardson and Bell are already dead. That leaves Morgan and Jefferson. Whoever the murderer is, you've got to believe
~~~~

Morgan and Jefferson could be his next targets. We're planning on getting warrants for both of them, but in the meantime, we'd like officers to shadow them until we can get those warrants."

"No way am I pulling two of my officers for full time surveillance but let me think about it. I may be able to shake loose a patrolman to make periodic checks on those two. That will have to do, detectives."

Both Adam and Marcus considered Boyer's decision to be myopic but left without saying another word.

Back at their desks, Adam slumped into his seat. "I'm not sure whether Boyer has it in for us or is just plain incompetent."

"Both if you ask me," Marcus quickly answered.

They arranged for forensics to email Detective Wrigley the results of their investigation at Richardson's house. O'Sullivan was asked to send the autopsy results, and Steve promised to send copies of the flash drive containing the spreadsheets.

Once they were assured Morgan and Jefferson would at least be somewhat protected and confident everyone was in the loop, they finished preparing the warrants and affidavits for the two doctors. The documents were dropped off at the courthouse for Judge Roberts to sign Monday morning. They left to interview Kyle Perry and Sylvia Porter—hoping the two had information that would help identify who wanted Richardson and Bell dead.

CHAPTER SIX

IT WAS ALMOST noon when Adam and Marcus arrived at Kyle Perry's condo on James Island. Mira Vista was a gated community, but their standard-issue police transponder allowed Adam to open the gate. Perry's unit was on the second floor. Marcus knocked and the door slowly opened—security chain still attached.

"Yes?"

"Are you Kyle Perry?" Adam questioned.

"Yes."

"Mr. Perry, I'm Detective Adam Stone." He showed his shield. "This is Detective Williams. We'd like a few words with you."

"About what?"

"We have a few questions concerning Dr. Charles Richardson. We understand he treated you."

It was clear the name had a profound effect. Perry's head dropped slightly, and Adam could see disgust on his face. Perry quickly recovered. "Hang on." He released the chain and opened the door.

Adam judged Perry to be in his early thirties. He wore jeans and a dress shirt with the sleeves rolled up. He had short hair and a neatly trimmed beard. There was a reading light and a book open on an end table next to a couch. The condo was small and sparsely furnished—what furniture there was looked fairly commonplace, and there were a few framed prints of generic beach scenes on the walls. It seemed apparent that Perry lived alone.

Adam and Marcus settled on the couch, and Perry sat in a chair across from them. "Tell us about Doctor Richardson," Adam said.

"Why? That was a long time ago."

"Well, we're primarily concerned with the oxycodone he supplied."

Perry again lowered his head and was quiet for a moment. He finally said, "I'm not sure I want to discuss my medical history, detectives. Why don't you just tell me why you're here."

"Fair enough," Adam offered. "We're investigating the deaths of Dr. Richardson and one of his associates, Dr. Nathan Bell. Both doctors were recently murdered, and we're in the process of interviewing some of their patients."

Perry took several deep breaths trying to deal with what he'd just heard. "Okay, I was treated by Dr. Richardson about four years ago."

"Mr. Perry," Marcus said, "we know about your use and abuse of opioids you obtained from Richardson. We also know you spent time in prison. We're not here to judge or charge you with criminal activity. We're only looking for information that can help with our murder investigations. Why don't you start by telling us why you first saw Dr. Richardson?"

After hesitating a moment, Perry agreed. "Back in 2016, I was injured while playing softball. I tore my ACL and required extensive reconstructive surgery. I don't know if you're familiar with that type of surgery, but my recovery was extremely painful and required extended physical therapy to regain the use of my leg. At that time, I was an attorney at Jones, Sanders, and Cole. I was one of only two junior associates there and working seventy hours a week. I missed a few weeks of work after the surgery and couldn't afford to miss anymore." Perry's voice took on a sarcastic tone when he continued. "If I did, I'd be fired, or as they put it, 'I would be happier at a smaller firm.'"

Adam glanced at Marcus and said, "We're very familiar with Jones, Sanders, and Cole, and we know how they treat their associates. Please go ahead."

"I went to Dr. Richardson for my rehab program. He started with some pretty intensive therapy. I was still in a lot of pain, and he prescribed pills to help when I returned to work. The workload at the firm was extreme, and it got tougher and tougher to make it. I needed five or six pills to get through the 16-hour days. Pretty soon that increased to ten or twelve pills. I think you get the picture. It didn't take long before I was hooked, and that's when he told me he couldn't increase my prescription but did have a private source he was willing to give me. The only catch was that they were very expensive, and I'd have to pay cash. No way was I going to get as much OXY as I needed anywhere else, so I paid. You can imagine what happened to my performance at the firm. It took a dive along with my bank account.

"Finally, I got fired. I was out of work, out of money, and addicted to fucking pills. My mom and dad took me in, but I did what most junkies do. I stole from my family and started breaking into houses. It didn't take long before I got caught. That's a Class D felony, and I got two years in Kershaw Correctional. The only good thing about prison is that it got me clean. I kept my head down, did my time, and got paroled after a little over a year.

"So, I get out. I'm an ex-con, got no money, no law license, and no job. I worked at a landscaping company for about six months. My parents helped out as much as they could. I could barely afford a place to live and put food on the table—but never missed an AA meeting and stayed clean. That's when I ran into Ted Samuels. I went to law school with Ted at USC. He wasn't the sharpest pencil in the pouch, but he was a nice guy, and I helped him with some of our classes.

"We had coffee one afternoon at the Starbucks on Folly Road. We must have talked for hours. I told him what happened to me. He didn't judge—he just listened. And then he asked me to come work for him. He had a small family practice right down the road on Folly."

"But you lost your license, right?" Marcus questioned.

"Right, but I can still do research and write briefs. That's what I do there. We handle mostly divorces, wills, and family stuff like that. He couldn't afford to pay me much, but I didn't care. There's no way I could ever pay him back for what he's done for me. I'm at peace with where I am now in my life." He let out a long sigh. "That's pretty much it. Anything else you want to know?"

"Just one thing, and you know we've got to ask. Where were you this past Friday night?"

Perry shook his head. "Yeah, I get it, but no, detective, I didn't kill Dr. Richardson. I left the law firm about 6:00, went for a five-mile run, watched T.V., and went to bed around 10:00. Never left my apartment."

"All right, Mr. Perry. We don't need to know anything else from you now," Marcus said. "You should be proud of what you've accomplished. The only thing we may want you to do is to testify if our investigation ever makes it to court. Would you be willing to do that?"

"If it would help save one person from going through what I went through, you're damn right I'd do it."

The detectives stood and shook Perry's hand. Marcus gave him his card and said, "If you ever need anything, you give me a call."

They left the condo and were quiet as they drove toward Sylvia Porter's home in Hanahan.

A few minutes in, Marcus said, "I think if Richardson wasn't already dead, I'd like to kick the shit out of the fucker!"

Adam was surprised at the comment—not so much at the violence but the language. Marcus almost never swore—much less used the F-word.

They arrived at the Porters' address on Hawthorne Street twenty minutes later. The houses in the area were large, and the neighborhood impressive. Marcus tried the door, but no one answered. He knocked again with the same result.

He checked his watch. "Come on, we can check back later."

They were walking back to the Charger when they heard, "Hello there." An older woman was standing on the porch next door. "Are you looking for Mr. Porter?"

"Actually, we're here to see Sylvia Porter," Adam answered.

"Oh dear, Sylvia hasn't been there for a few months."

Adam and Marcus approached the woman. "Do you know when Mr. Porter might be back?" Adam asked.

"Well, it's Sunday, and I imagine Kurt's still at church. I'd expect he'd be back any time now."

"Thank you, ma'am. We'll stop back in a while. You have a nice day."

They were almost back to the Charger when a Ford Blazer pulled into the driveway. They made their way back to the house as a middle-aged man got out and said, "Can I help you?"

"Yes, sir. I'm Detective Stone and this is my partner, Detective Williams. We were looking for Sylvia. Do you know how we might get in touch with her?"

"I'm Sylvia's father. What do you want with her?"

"Sir, may we come in and speak with you?" Marcus offered.

"Not until I know what this is about."

"We'd like to ask about a former doctor of hers—Charles Richardson."

"Sylvia has nothing to say about that son of a bitch," Porter said, the hostility in his voice evident.

"Mr. Porter," Adam said, "we can appreciate your feelings toward that man. But Dr. Richardson was recently murdered, and we believe Sylvia may be able to help in our investigation. May we please come in and talk?"

Porter was quiet for a moment and then said, "All right. I suppose so." Adam and Marcus followed him into the house. "Have a seat, detectives. Sorry about the way I acted. Can I get you something to drink?"

"No thank you, sir," Marcus said. "Where is Sylvia now? Would it be possible for us to speak with her?"

"Before I say anything more, what is it exactly you want to know?"

"That's understandable," Marcus continued. "The simple answer is that Dr. Richardson was murdered early Saturday morning, and we have reason to believe he was involved in the illegal distribution of opioids. We're hoping your daughter might give us information about that. Sylvia isn't in any trouble."

Porter shook his head. "Not in any trouble? Well, I don't think you understand what that man did to her."

"That's what we're here to find out, Mr. Porter. Is your wife available to join us?"

"We're divorced. She lives in Seattle."

"I'm sorry," Marcus said.

"Don't be. She's been out of the picture for ten years now. I was one of the chief engineers for Boeing out in Washington and transferred here when the new plant opened in 2009. We were having problems even back then and decided to call it quits. I got custody of Sylvia. Now, what is it you want to know about her?"

"Like I said, we know your daughter was Richardson's patient. I assume she was injured. What happened?"

Porter was beginning to calm down. "Listen, detectives, it's not easy for me to talk about Richardson."

"We can appreciate that," Marcus said. "Please tell us about Sylvia's injury."

He collected himself and continued, "Sylvia was a straight A student and an excellent soccer player at Hanahan High School. During the season, she began complaining about pain in her back and legs. It got to the point where our doctor ordered an MRI which showed multiple herniated discs. The discs had degenerated to the point where they were basically bone on bone, and there wasn't much choice but to operate. One of the discs was removed and the others fused together to stabilize the spine. She was in the hospital for two nights and discharged with a prescription for 30 oxycodone pills. She had a tough time after the surgery, and before we knew it she was out of the pills. She was given several more prescriptions. After about a month or so, she started physical therapy."

The story hit Adam hard. His own daughter played high school soccer and was an "A" student.

"Why did you choose Dr. Richardson?" Adam asked.

He hung his head and shook it. "The location was just the most convenient. Wish I could … but anyway, she started going to PRO Care twice a week. She seemed to be getting better, and Richardson said he might send her to a doctor named Bell for follow up treatments. I thought she was off the pills by then. What I didn't know was that Richardson was still giving Sylvia prescriptions for more pain pills. I was naïve enough to think a doctor wouldn't do that to a child. Apparently, he continued to up the strength and number of pills she was taking. It didn't take long before she was addicted, and I still didn't know. I found out later that's when he offered her stronger pills. The only catch was that she needed to pay cash because those pills were 'off-the-books.' This way he didn't have to report those pills he sold for cash. Pretty soon her grades started going down. She was losing weight and always seemed tired. I was concerned, and that's when I first found pills she'd hidden in her dresser. Yeah, I went through her things. I wish to hell I'd done it sooner."

"What did she say when you confronted her?"

"She denied it. She told me she'd forgotten they were even there. Around then, I noticed that my Rolex and diamond cufflinks were gone. Other things started disappearing. I was so naïve. It just didn't occur to me that my little girl could be stealing from me. Finally, when my wedding ring went missing, I confronted her again."

"What happened this time?" Adam asked.

Porter's eyes were beginning to water. "She said it was none of my business. I told her I'd get her help. She asked me for money, and when I refused, she left the house. She didn't come home that night or the next three. Then I got a call from my ex. Sylvia had called her and said I was in trouble, and she needed my wife to Western Union her a thousand dollars.

"That night I tore Sylvia's room apart and found a book of matches with *Christy's Lounge* on it. I looked it up—it's a strip club. I went there that night and waited outside the place. After a while, this car pulls in the lot. Two guys get out of the front, and Sylvia and another girl get out of the back. I got out and grabbed her, and that's when one of the guys pulled a knife. I took care of the guy with the knife and managed to get Sylvia into the Blazer."

"What do you mean you took care of him?" questioned Adam.

"I used to be an Army Ranger working counterinsurgency in Iraq and Yemen, detective. Believe me—he was no problem. To make a long story short, I was able to get Sylvia into rehab in North Carolina. She was there for two months at $30,000 a month. When she got out, she was home a month before she relapsed. She's been in a facility outside Jacksonville for the last month and a half. That one's $40,000 a month. She seems to be doing much better, but who knows."

"We're sorry you had to go through that," Adam said. "How long do you expect she'll stay there?"

"I don't know. They said they'd give a recommendation in a few weeks. I hope to hell this one sticks. I've had to take a second mortgage on my house. I'll do what I need to do, but it's tough."

"For the record, we just have to ask where you were this last Friday night," Adam said.

Porter seemed surprised by the question, but quickly answered, "Right here. Left work around 7:30, stopped at the Taphouse on Greenridge for dinner, and spent the rest of the night at home."

"All right, Mr. Porter, and thanks for your help. We hope everything works out this time." Adam gave Porter his card. "Give me a call if you can think of anything else that might help."

A strange smile appeared on Porter's face. "The only thing that helps is knowing Richardson is dead."

CHAPTER SEVEN

THE INTERVIEWS WITH Perry and Porter's father took most of the afternoon, and now it was Marcus' turn to struggle staying awake. Adam suggested he head home to see Makayla and catch a few hours of sleep. He'd remain at Lockwood updating Richardson's murder book and get one started for Nathan Bell. He'd also take another shot at the spreadsheets on the flash drive and follow up on Richardson's final autopsy report plus whatever information Mt. Pleasant may have sent on the Bell murder.

After dropping off Marcus at the station, Adam realized he hadn't eaten since he had one of Tracy's sandwiches at three that morning. He had plenty of work to do but needed a quick break to recharge. He grabbed the folder Steve had prepared on the three doctors and made the short drive to Rutledge Cab Company, a cop bar a mile or so from Lockwood. He didn't frequent the bar that often—he'd heard most all the cop stories several times and wasn't interested in the badge bunnies who hung around looking to hook up with a cop. But the food was good, and he did enjoy seeing some of his friends outside the confines of the station.

He ordered a burger and coffee and ate while reviewing the files. An hour later, he was back at Lockwood.

Being Sunday evening, only two other detectives were pulling duty in the bullpen. Richardson's autopsy report wasn't finished, and Detective Wrigley hadn't yet sent anything on Bell. Adam spent an hour or so researching the opioid trade and working on Bell's murder book. He was making notes on the position of Nathan Bell's body when he decided to check the FBI's Uniform Crime Reporting (UCR) Program. The UCR Program's supplementary homicide data provides information regarding the age, sex, race, and ethnicity of the murder victim and the offender; the type of weapon used; the relationship of the victim to the offender; and the circumstance surrounding the incident. Law enforcement agencies across the country are asked to provide this supplementary homicide data for each murder they report to the UCR Program.

Adam logged into the UCR's Supplementary Homicide Report looking for murders where the victim was positioned in the same way Nathan Bell's body was found. There were several hits beginning in the 90s with the murder of four people in a Las Vegas hotel. All the bodies had been positioned as if lying in a casket. None of the murders was ever solved. It was almost midnight, and he was starting to make notes of additional murders matching his parameters when the call came in. It was Tracy.

"Tracy, is everything okay?" He was definitely concerned. She never called when he was working unless something was wrong.

"No, Adam, it's not okay!"

"What happened? Is Piper all right?"

"Piper's fine," Tracy assured him. "We were both asleep when Max started barking and woke me up. I got downstairs, turned on the porch light, and must have scared whoever was out there because he dropped something and ran across the parking lot. He jumped into a car and drove away so fast the tires smoked. Piper came downstairs, and we went outside and found a spray-paint can and saw what he did."

"What? What did he do!"

"There are numbers painted on the front door and under the window."

"Numbers? What numbers?"

"It's hard to make out. 10-105, I think, on the door."

Adam froze—10-105 was the Charleston police code for reporting a dead body.

"What about the window?"

"Yes." Her voice was shaking now. "10-82. What does all this mean, Adam?"

"Listen to me," Adam ordered, "do not touch that spray can. Lock the doors and stay away from the windows. Call 911. I'll be there as soon as I can."

Adam opened his desk drawer and grabbed his Glock. He was out of the station and speeding over the James Island connector minutes later. His breathing was rapid, and he felt his hands beginning to shake. *Damn it!* Someone had just spray-painted police codes on the front of his apartment. And the message was clear—10-105 meant a dead body, and 10-82 meant a rape victim.

He hit 90 going across the connector and skidded off Maybank into his apartment complex less than ten minutes after leaving the station. The graffiti brought bile to his mouth as he stared for a raging moment at the all too familiar police codes before rushing into the house. Once inside, he hugged Piper and Tracy. They looked terrified. He too felt a wave of terror run through him.

Tracy was holding the phone and told Adam the 911 operator was still on the line.

Adam grabbed the phone. "This is Detective Adam Stone. This call was made from my apartment. Where's the response!"

The 911 operator remained calm. "Detective, officers have been dispatched and should be there any minute now. Please confirm there are no injuries at the scene."

"Confirmed," Adam responded. Headlights appeared outside the apartment. "Okay, the patrol car just arrived. Thanks for your help." He disconnected the line and opened the front door. He recognized one of the officers approaching and shouted, "Levins, this is my place."

Officer Levins nodded and asked, "Is everyone all right, sir?"

"Hell no!" Adam was showing them the graffiti when Levins' partner bent down to pick up the spray can.

"Don't touch that! That goes in a fucking evidence bag."

Clearly embarrassed, the officer quickly replied "Yes, sir. Sorry, sir."

Another patrol car arrived as the red-faced officer left to retrieve an evidence bag. Adam turned to Levins and said, "As soon as a detective gets here have him call me at Lockwood."

Adam went back inside and told Tracy and Piper he was going back to the station. "Listen, I'm going to have officers posted outside for the rest of the night. You're going to be all right tonight." He turned his attention to Piper. "Piper, I want you to pack some things in the morning. You're going to Tracy's house tomorrow." He looked at Tracy. "I'll have an officer stationed outside your place."

"Adam, why is this happening again? Are these the same people that hurt Marcus?"

"No."

"Daddy, I'm scared," Piper said.

Adam pulled her close. "I know, baby. Don't worry. Nothing's going to happen to you and Grandma. I promise. I've got to go now." Adam again told them to try and get some sleep even though he knew that wasn't going to happen.

He'd retrieved the evidence bag containing the paint can and was heading back to the station when his cell rang. It was Marcus. "What's going on? I just got back to Lockwood, and they're telling me someone hit your apartment tonight."

"Yeah, something like that. I'll be back in a few minutes. Is there anyone there to run an AFIS? I need a fingerprint scan off a can of spray paint I'm bringing in."

"I think so, but I'll check. Listen, tell me what's …"

Adam disconnected the call and thought to himself, *Here we fucking go again.* When Marcus was attacked by men from the Sinaloa Cartel earlier that year, Piper had to move in with Tracy, and an officer stayed with them until the Posse's Spider Gomez and the cartel's Miguel Alvarez were killed.

Adam arrived at Lockwood five minutes later, and Marcus was waiting for him in the bullpen. "For Christ's sake, Adam. Are you going to tell me what happened?"

Adam told him about the spray-painted numbers, and the bile rushed back up his throat.

"God, Adam," Marcus said, "they're targeting Piper too."

"Don't you think I know that!" Adam took a deep breath. "Sorry, brother. I can't believe this shit is happening again.".

"I hear you. Who do you think did it?"

"No question who's behind it," Adam replied. "It's got to be the Posse. It's been a while since we took out Spider, and they lost their hold on the heroin trade, and that wasn't the first time we busted up one of their major deals. You've got to figure they're trying to reestablish themselves. Lucas Vicario is their new shot caller, and he needs to prove he can run the show. And he's apparently naïve enough to think that threatening us is somehow going to accomplish that."

"Probably, but this might have to do with our murder investigation."

"Well, there's one way to find out. For starters, we'll run prints on the can."

"Come on," Marcus said, "I found a tech who can lift the prints and run them through the AFIS database." Adam followed Marcus downstairs to the biometric lab and gave the bag to the tech on duty. He logged it in and said he'd have something in about thirty minutes.

"Come on, Adam. Let's go upstairs and get some coffee."

Adam checked his watch—almost 3:00 in the morning. "You go ahead. I need to take off for an hour or two. Call me as soon as you get the lab result."

"Where're you going?"

"I want to check on the family and see if Chester Wood knows why I got hit tonight and Santoro's pill business. Oh, and I completely forgot. I ran an UCR search of murders matching the position we found Bell in. I got several hits, but then the call came in about the graffiti. We need to get back on that as soon as I get back."

"You're seeing Wood? It's the middle of the night!"

"Trust me, Marcus, Chester doesn't sleep."

After checking in on Piper and Tracy, Adam made the twenty-minute drive across town to North Charleston's old Navy Shipyards.

Most cops working the street for any length of time develop undercover informants. These "snitches" often provide valuable information and are coveted by their handlers. Adam had his own stable of snitches. Chester Wood was one of his most valuable.

Wood lived in the dark side of the web—more often than not working for various elements of organized crime in Charleston. Years ago, Adam had kept Chester out of a bust, and by doing so, added a world-class computer hacker to his stable of snitches.

Chester and his squirrely little girlfriend, Nora, lived near the abandoned Navy Shipyards in an old bodega that had been converted into a one-bedroom apartment. Adam never bothered to check whether they were at their place—they almost never left.

The streets were virtually deserted when Adam parked his Charger across from Chester's. His footsteps echoed off the pavement as a black cat dashed across the street and leaped into the field next to the building. A faint light shone behind one of the grime-covered, barred windows weeping rust. Adam hit the steel door with the back of his fist.

A moment later he heard a high-pitched voice say, "Who's there?"

"Nora, open the door."

Adam could hear several locks being unlocked, and the door opened.

Nora turned around and called out, "Hey, Chester. There's some weird-looking guy here to see you."

"Knock it off, Nora," Adam mumbled as he brushed past her.

"Bite me, Stone."

The cramped living room was lit by the pale blue light emanating from a large lava lamp resting on a small metal table next to a red beanbag chair. The rest of the living room was filled with electronic equipment haphazardly connected by a myriad of cables crisscrossing the floor. Chester Wood sat behind one of the three computer monitors—its light illuminating his thin face shielded by a shabby hooded sweatshirt. A liter of Diet Pepsi was next to him. Star Wars figurines—Darth Vader, Luke Skywalker, Chewbacca, R2-D2, others—lined a long a wooden shelf behind him. A Baby Yoda doll was clipped to the monitor in front of him.

Adam made his way through the cables and said, "Chester, I need information."

"Gee, what a surprise," Nora whined. "Detective Stone needs information."

"Shut up, Nora," Chester said. "It's been a while, Stone. What'd you need this time?"

"Who the hell spray painted a murder and rape threat on my home? Did the Posse and Lucas Vicario do this?"

"I haven't heard anything about any spray painted threat. But as far as the Posse goes—Vicario's not the smartest shot caller out there, but he's definitely one of the most ruthless. The Posse's reputation took a major hit when Spider was killed, and they lost the Cartel's heroin business. Word is he'd do almost anything to get their rep and that business back. But there's a faction inside the gang that isn't all that happy with the way he's running things."

Adam was certainly aware of Vicario's reputation but was unaware that his power might be challenged. "Is Vicario still solid?"

"Yeah, but he thinks he needs to do something to show he can handle things."

"Do something as in what?"

"Don't know," Chester replied, "but you were one of the reasons the Posse lost its rep. If I were you, I'd watch my back."

"I'll do that. Now, tell me about who's pushing pills around here and how they're doing it."

Chester took the next few minutes telling Adam pretty much everything he'd already heard from Terry Blackwood about the distribution of opioids. Nick Santoro's group controlled most of the business, and they were in the process of getting rid of the smaller competition.

"We heard Santoro's getting his product from China, and it's being supplied out of Chicago," Adam said.

"Your source is good. Think about it. Most smaller pushers are getting their stuff out of Mexico—just like that doctor that was murdered. And here's something I bet your friends down at Lockwood don't know."

"What's that?"

Chester thought for a moment before answering. "Nora and I have been a little short lately. How about you give me a couple hundred for the info? Believe me, it's worth it."

"You want money? I'll tell you what, Chester. Instead of money, maybe I'll make a call to Mr. Santoro and tell him about all the wonderful information you've been giving me all these years. How's that sound?"

"All right, all right! Take it easy, Stone. I was just asking."

"Well, don't ask. Now, tell me what I don't know."

"The Sinaloa Cartel is finished dealing with the Posse. They've been burned twice in major deals with them. And in addition to the cartel losing millions of dollars of product, don't forget Miguel Alvarez and several of his soldiers were killed in the process."

"I know all that."

"I'm not finished, Stone. Things are going to change, and I hear from my sources that the cartel is talking with Nick Santoro about giving his organization their heroin distribution business in Charleston."

"I suppose that makes sense," Adam said.

"Damn right it makes sense. The Sinaloa Cartel isn't in the pill business, but opioid addiction is good for them—pill junkies eventually move on to heroin."

Now the picture was clear to Adam. First, Nick Santoro takes out his OXY competition and makes a deal with the cartel for their heroin trade. If he can pull it off, his organization will control the addicts from pills to the hard stuff. Santoro's mob already controls most of the prostitution, gambling, and loansharking. A hell of a business strategy.

"All right, Chester. Keep me informed if you hear anything else."

~~~~

Marcus was at his desk when Adam returned to the station.

"Any word on the prints?" Adam asked.
~~~~

"Yeah. I called you, but you didn't answer. We got a full and a 20-point partial hit on a Jimmy Moreno. He's done time for possession with intent to sell. He's Posse."

"I figured that."

"Let's bring him in."

"Not yet. I don't want Vicario knowing what we know. Plus, a misdemeanor vandalism charge isn't going to do us any good."

"Probably right. So what did Chester say?"

"Word is Vicario is ready to do almost anything to get the Posse's reputation back. We need to talk to Merchant about more protection for our families."

"Agreed," Marcus said. "Anything else?"

Adam passed on the information confirming Nick Santoro's move to eliminate the OXY competition and his discussions with the Sinaloa Cartel to take over the distribution of their supply of heroin.

"Right," Marcus replied, "I agree Nick Santoro's our prime suspect in both the Richardson and Bell murders. But I'm not ready to give Sylvia Porter's father a complete pass on Richardson's murder. Remember Kurt Porter was an Army Ranger, and he said the only thing that made him feel better was knowing Richardson was dead."

"True enough, but what about Dr. Bell's murder? Sylvia was never his patient."

"You're right, but that still doesn't mean Porter couldn't have got to Richardson before Santoro took out Bell—if he actually ordered the hit."

"I think that's a stretch, partner," Adam replied. "Nick Santoro as definitely our prime, but we'll leave Porter in the mix for the time being. But what about Kyle Perry? He lost everything and did time because of what Richardson did to him."

"I don't think so," Marcus offered. "Granted Richardson almost destroyed Perry's life, but Perry played a part in his own addiction. Whatever the case, it sounded like he'd moved on."

"You're probably right, but let's not write him off just yet."

"All right," agreed Marcus, "but since we're talking about possible suspects, how about the other two doctors: Morgan and Jefferson. Maybe one of them got greedy and took out Richardson and Bell."

"Possibly, but again, that's a stretch. I can see them screwing their patients, but murder? I don't think so."

"Well, I agree it's a longshot, but Judge Roberts should approve the warrants for their homes and offices this morning. We'll get a better idea when we talk to them. Did you come up with anything while I was at Chester's place?"

"As a matter of fact, I did. I decided to take another look at the spreadsheets. Something just didn't seem to add up."

"I'm listening," Adam said. "Go ahead."

"Okay, so bear with me. Richardson and those three doctors had to be working by themselves. There's no way they could have kept their pill business quiet if they'd been in a group practice with multiple doctors and support staffs. And all those docs only had one assistant. You've got to believe they were in on the scheme."

"I'm with you so far," Adam said.

"I did some research and learned that a single doctor sees an average of fifteen to twenty patients a day. I'm also assuming that most of their patients were legit, and a good portion were prescribed nonnarcotic medications—you know for migraines, nerve pain, stuff like that. Maybe Richardson's three doctors had two or three 'off the books' addicts they were supplying every day. If they sell a hundred pills to each of them at $10 or $20 a pill, that works out to somewhere in the neighborhood of $150,000 or $200,000 a month."

"Sounds about right."

"The combined monthly totals on that main spreadsheet were consistently over $500,000. Something doesn't add up."

"So, what are you saying?" Adam asked.

A sly smile spread across Marcus' face. "You ever heard of Amway?"

"Sure, it's a pyramid scheme." And then it hit him. "Jesus, Marcus. Why didn't I see it? I think you might be right. Each one of those doctors had their own group of doctors they were supplying. This thing could be bigger than we thought!"

"Exactly," Marcus said. "And if you wanted to take out the whole pyramid, eliminate Richardson and his three main suppliers."

Adam looked at his watch and saw it was almost 7:00 am. "Come on, we need to talk to Merchant."

CHAPTER EIGHT

THE CHIEF HAD just set down his morning coffee and taken off his suit jacket when Adam and Marcus appeared at his door.

"Good morning, detectives. How's the Richardson investigation going?"

"That's why we're here," Adam began. He then explained their belief that Santoro was eliminating the smaller pill dealers and was in talks with the Sinaloa Cartel to take over distribution of their heroin supply in Charleston.

"I hate to say it, but Santoro's moves make sense for his organization," Merchant admitted. "I assume you're now convinced he's behind the murder of the two doctors, right?"

"Yes, sir," Marcus answered. "I'd say Santoro's our prime suspect, but there's also the father of a patient Richardson got hooked on OXY. His name is Kurt Porter. It's a long shot, but we're also looking at the possibility that one of the other two doctors might have killed Richardson and Bell in order to take over the operation."

"How do you want to proceed?"

"We're collecting a good amount of evidence proving Richardson and the other three doctors were running a sort of pyramid scheme selling drugs. And it seems clear from crime scene evidence that Bell and Richardson were murdered by the same person. The problem is we've got nothing solid pointing to the killer."

"And you think the other two doctors are next on the killer's list?"

"We do."

"Do you want to bring them in?"

"No. We'd like to set up surveillance on those doctors. If the killer comes after them like we think he will, it's our best chance of nailing him. We'll have warrants for both of them and can move on them if we need to."

Merchant said nothing for a moment. He was digesting the information. "All right. At this point, I don't think there's a better option. Set up surveillance from 6:00 pm to 6:00 am. This will put pressure on our manpower, but it's our best approach. And I want you coordinating this with Boyer."

"Yes, sir," Adam said. "There's something else."

"And that is?"

Adam explained the situation with Vicario, the weakened Posse, and the graffiti at his apartment. "Marcus and I are spending all our time in the field or at the station. Our families are vulnerable. I'm moving Piper into Ann's mother's house like I did last year."

Marcus jumped in to say how effective Officers Rodriguez and Fitzgerald were in their posts after he'd been attacked by the cartel.

"Consider it done," Merchant quickly agreed. "But you'll also need to run that through the chain of command."

Adam and Marcus looked at each other—their frustration obvious.

Merchant smiled and said, "Yeah, I know. Frank can be an ass at times."

They answered in unison, "Yes, he can."

"Thank you, Ed." Adam said.

They were at the door but turned back when Merchant called out. "And detectives, you didn't hear that last comment about our new captain. Right?"

Adam smiled. "We don't know what you're talking about, Chief."

~~~~

They took the information Gagyi had prepared on doctors Morgan and Jefferson and left for Boyer's office. His door was open. "Captain, can we have a minute with you?" Adam asked.

"Sure but make it quick."

"Of course," Adam said and laid it all out—the list of suspects and the graffiti attack at his apartment, but of course Boyer bitched and moaned about being understaffed and the
~~~~

overtime cost. However, because the suggestion had come from Merchant, he could do little to thwart the requests and said he take care of it.

Back at their desks, Adam suggested they go ahead and push to get search warrants for the doctors' offices and homes. They'd protect them for now, but that didn't mean they wouldn't be prosecuted for their part in the narcotics operation.

It was approaching noon, and Marcus suggested they grab a bite at the Cab Company and continue discussing the case over lunch.

After ordering their food, Marcus said, "You know, Adam, I've been thinking."

Adam grinned. "Well, that's promising."

Marcus returned the smile. "Yeah, right. Listen. Let's say you're Dr. Richardson. What's the biggest problem you've got with the OXY scheme you're running?"

"Getting shot?" Adam quickly answered.

"Sure, there's that. But what about all that cash you're collecting?"

"You're right. No way can he put even a fraction of the cash in the bank. The feds would be all over him. He's got to launder it, or at least keep it until he can get it out of the country."

"Precisely," Marcus said. "It's a cash business—just like prostitution, gambling, and loansharking. Remember the key we found in Richardson's safe, with the number on it? Maybe it's to a safety deposit box."

"No. Ann and I had one at Wells Fargo, and those bank keys don't look anything like the one in the safe. Plus, safety deposit boxes aren't going to hold that much cash. What else could it be for?"

"A storage locker?" Marcus offered. "One of those 'U-Store-It' places. Makayla and I have a bunch of our stuff in one called CubeSmart on Dorchester."

"Let me check something." Adam pulled out his phone. He opened Safari and punched in "storage, 29401," Richardson's zip. Five locations on the peninsula popped up.

The waitress brought their sandwiches and after she left, Adam said, "Enjoy your lunch, partner. We need to get that key out of evidence and hit the pavement this afternoon!"

"Hold your horses. We'll need a search warrant to access one of those units. No way is Roberts going to issue a warrant unless we give him a specific storage company, locker number, and a darn good reason we think there's evidence inside."

"So, what do we do?"

"Let's check those five locations on the Peninsula. When we find unit 128, we try the key. If it works, we don't open it, not until we get that warrant."

"I guess you're right. Just a hell of a lot of shit to go through."

"It is," Marcus agreed, "but you know we got to play the game. Let's just finish lunch, get the fricking key, and go on a treasure hunt."

They spent much of the afternoon checking out each of the downtown storage unit locations. After striking out at all five locations, Adam muttered, "Well, that was a wild goose chase, and the goose got away!"

Both detectives were disappointed, but Marcus wasn't ready to give up on the storage unit idea. "If I were Richardson, I'd buy jewelry or other stuff that could be stored there and sold later. Heck, Adam, nowadays you can sell almost anything online. If that storage unit isn't on the Peninsula, it's probably close to his office. Hang on a second." Marcus brought up a map of storage locations near PRO Care. There were seven locations fairly close by. He swung the monitor around so Adam could see the map.

"Let's plan on checking those out tomorrow morning," Marcus suggested. "We can start with the closest to his office and work outward."

"All right," agreed Adam, "but I still think it's a longshot. Plus, how's that going to help us identify Richardson's and Bell's killer?"

~~~~

As promised, the information on Bell's murder arrived earlier that afternoon from Detective Wrigley. The tox screen found no narcotics residue in his blood. He was a pusher—not a user.

No fingerprints other than Bell's were found at the scene. But a security tape included in Wrigley's package showed what looked like a man in a hooded sweatshirt approaching Bell's front door at 3:46 the morning of his murder. The person took less than a minute to pick the lock on the front door and enter
~~~~

the condo. He reappeared 45 minutes later and ducked around the building out of camera range. His face was obscured by the hood, but Adam noticed a crucial detail—the person had a slight but recognizable limp.

"I don't think we had any doubt that whoever killed Bell also murdered Richardson, but this confirms it," Adam said. "I bet he picked Richardson's front door. Plus, the guy wore a hooded sweatshirt and walked with a limp—just like at Richardson's."

The detectives were continuing to analyze the data when Marcus suddenly stopped. "Jesus, Adam, listen to this!" He began reading a passage from Bell's autopsy report. "'A small portion of granule material was recovered from the bed sheets adjacent to the victim's left shoulder. Laboratory analysis identified the material to be silicon dioxide ($SiO2$) ranging in size between approximately 80 and 300 microns. The recovered material looks to be standard play sand.'"

"The same stuff we found on Richardson!" Adam said. "What the hell is kid's sand doing at both murder scenes? Let's search the UCR again but add the presence of sand along with the positioning of the body. I figure the only reason Richardson's body wasn't in the same position as Bell's is that he heard that dog barking and took off before he could position him. But he did do the sand thing, right?"

The search generated around twenty more murders from the 90s through 2014 that matched the new parameters—all the victims had underworld ties and the killer was never found. But before Adam could say anything, his cell rang.

Adam held up his hand and answered, "Detective Stone."

"Stone, it's Blackwood. Can you talk?"

"Sure, Marcus is here. I'll put you on speaker."

"Don't!"

"All right. Go ahead. What's up?"

Blackwood's voice dropped to a near whisper. "Right. So, I'm at Cutty's tonight doing a few shots and shooting the shit with one of my Santoro contacts. The guy's been part of the family's business well before Santoro took over. He'd been at it all night and was wasted. I mean this guy was three sheets. I start hinting that I'm feeling like shit and could use something to smooth things out. Now, get this. He starts rambling on about pills and your two doctors that got shot. I couldn't believe it. I mean the old guy's ready to pass out, and I swear to God he smiles at me and says, 'It's like the Sandman's come to town.'"

"What does that mean?"

"I had no idea. So I call Mitch O'Shaughnessy. Remember him?"

"Yeah," Adam said, "homicide, right?"

"Exactly. He spent thirty years there. Retired four or five years ago. So I ask him if he knows who this Sandman is, and he tells me it's probably this old hitman the Chicago mob used to use on high priority targets. Mitch thinks he's one of those urban legends because he's never been caught, and no one knows much about the guy other than he was called the Sandman because he put people to sleep—like permanently."

"What else did O'Shaughnessy say about this Sandman guy?"

"Not much other than he was supposed to be some kind of psychopath, and nobody seems to know what he looks like."

"All right," Adam said. "You earned your stripes tonight, buddy. Watch your ass out there and let me know if you hear anything else."

Adam passed on the information to Marcus that Blackwood had given him.

"I got an idea," Adam offered. "Chief Taylor joined the department back in the mid-70s, right?"

"I think around 1974 or 1975," Marcus agreed.

"He might know something about the guy." Adam checked his watch. "It's only 9:45 p.m. Should we call him?"

"Do it."

~~~~

Adam placed the call to Chief Taylor. It rang and rang, and he was about to hang up when he heard, "Hello, Detective Stone."

"Good evening, Chief. I'm sorry to bother you this late."

"Don't be, son. I was just sitting here in my library reading one of those books I never had the time to read when we were chasing bad guys. What can I do for you?"

"Well, I'm here at the station with Marcus. I have you on speaker, and we have a few questions for you."

Taylor chuckled. "It's nice to know I haven't been forgotten already. Go ahead."
~~~~

Adam took a few minutes getting Taylor up to speed and then got right to it. "Chief, you were working homicide back in the late 70's and early 80's. Did you ever hear anything about this Sandman?"

Taylor didn't answer.

"Sir?"

"Hang on a second." Adam heard footsteps and a door closing. Then Taylor was back on the line. "Yes, I knew about the Sandman. To tell you the truth, back then most of us thought he was some kind of ghost. No one knew much about him. As you know, there were hundreds of mob-related contract murders in Chicago in the 70s and 80s. But in the early 90s, we started to hear the name, Sandman, but only if it was a really big hit on someone who double-crossed the Chicago mob."

"You think this guy's real?" Adam asked. "If he is, he's got to be in his seventies."

"I don't know for sure whether he's real or not. But I know that murder can sometimes become addictive for some of these contract killers. And I've known some of these hitmen that practice their trade well into their seventies. I know about your investigation into the murder of those two doctors, and I can tell you this; if he is real and in Charleston, you and Marcus had better be careful. With age comes experience—and experience in his profession can be deadly."

"Thanks again for the information. You have a good night, Chief."

Adam was about to hang up when Taylor said, "Hang on, Adam." They could hear rustling, and Taylor came back on the line with a number for them to write down. "That's the cell number for Chief James Walczak. He was the chief in one of Chicago's South Side precincts. He's retired like me, but I've worked with him in the past, and he may have more information on the Sandman and who's dealing OXY pills up there."

"Thanks, Chief. We'll give him a call."

Adam thanked the chief again before hanging up.

~~~~

"You know, I don't know what to make of this," Adam said. "I have a hard time believing this Sandman guy is some unstoppable killing machine—all those supposed mob murders without getting caught? They guy was limping. Did he hurt himself, or is he just old?"

"I hear you, brother. But there's not much more we can do tonight. Officers Rodriguez and Fitzgerald are probably already at our places. I say you go home and get a few hours of sleep and get back here around 1:00 or 2:00 in the morning. Then I'll head on home and do the same."

"All right. What about tomorrow?"

"Let's plan on seeing Morgan and Jefferson first thing in the morning. They're definitely in danger, and we need to get them some protection. Then we can check out those storage places around Richardson's office. Maybe we'll luck out."
~~~~

"We also need to call Chief Walczak in Chicago. He's bound to know Eddie Santoro and his South Side crew and have information on how they distribute those pills they get from China."

"Good idea. Now get the hell out of here and go home."

CHAPTER NINE

IT HAD BEEN three days since Charles Richardson's murder, and the pressure was mounting to find a break in the case.

"Hey, Adam, I know almost everything we've learned so far points to Nick Santoro ordering the murders of Richardson and Bell. I don't know. I just keep going back to the look on Kurt Porter's face. We've both seen that look more than once."

"Okay, I get what you're saying, but with everything going on, there's no way we're getting additional help babysitting Porter. Plus, both those murders looked like professional hits."

"Yeah, but don't forget he was an Army Ranger. Those guys didn't come home without blood on their hands."

"Maybe so, but our priority has got to be Santoro. Granted, if I were Porter, I'd believe Richardson deserved to get the shit beat out of him—but murder? I don't think so.

Now let's get out of here and check out Morgan and Jefferson."

About twenty minutes later, they arrived at Dr. Morgan's office—a single-story brick home that had been converted into a medical office. There was a simple weather-beaten sign in front of the building that read:

Samuel L. Morgan, M.D.
1347 Folly Road

Adam parked in the small lot, and they entered a fairly large waiting room that had been a living room at one time. Adam glanced down the hall and saw four rooms—one most likely Dr. Morgan's private office, two patient examination rooms, and the fourth a restroom.

A red-haired, narrow-faced woman with skin the color of November was on the phone at the reception desk. It was difficult to gauge her age, but she looked to be in her mid-to-late-thirties. She covered the mouthpiece and whispered, "Good morning, just give me a minute here." A moment later she cradled the phone again and asked, "And what can I do for you gentlemen?"

Before Adam could answer, a young man left one of the rear offices carrying a small white bag. He hurried by—averting his eyes as he passed the detectives.

"Now, what can I do for you?" the receptionist repeated.

"We'd like to speak to Dr. Morgan," Adam said.

She seemed a bit perturbed and asked if they would like to make an appointment.

"No, ma'am," Adam removed his shield and showed it to the woman. "I'm Detective Stone and this is Detective Williams. What's your name, ma'am?"

She seemed taken aback by the question but answered, "Martha Simpson."

"Thank you, Ms. Simpson. Now, if you will please tell Dr. Morgan we're waiting to see him."

"Well, I don't know. Dr. Morgan has several more appointments scheduled this morning. I'm sure I can fit you in early this afternoon?"

"No, Ms. Simpson, that's not going to work. We'll see him now. You can tell him that, or we will."

She frowned and answered with a curt, "Wait here." She returned a moment later and told the detectives to follow her to Dr. Morgan's office. She threw a vexatious look at Adam and left—shutting the door more loudly than necessary.

A minute later, the door opened, and Dr. Morgan entered.

He couldn't have been more than a few inches over five feet. He had an appreciable paunch and a hairline in retreat. A scowl was pasted on his face. "What's this all about, officers?"

"Please take a seat, Dr. Morgan. We've got a few questions for you."

Morgan remained standing—his voice defiant. "Questions about what?"

"About your relationship with doctors Charles Richardson and Nathan Bell. I trust you're aware both men have been murdered.

And you're likely aware that your relationship with Dr. Richardson puts you in a dangerous position."

Morgan remained intransigent. "Yes, I knew Dr. Richardson, but I don't know what I can do to help you."

"Let's cut the bullshit, doctor," Adam quickly replied. "We know about your oxycodone racket. If you cooperate with us, we're willing to offer you protection."

Morgan was taciturn, obviously considering his options. Finally, he said, "Are you going to charge me with a crime, detectives? If that's the case, you're going to have to talk to my attorney. If not, I have patients to see."

"At this point, Dr. Morgan, the decision is yours. But if you choose not to cooperate, we can't guarantee your safety."

Morgan walked to the door and opened it. "We're finished here. I'll need you to leave."

Adam removed one of his cards and placed it on Morgan's desk. "I suggest you reconsider."

"Leave!" Morgan repeated.

Back in the car, Adam said, "I thought doctors are supposed to be smart. I don't think Morgan realizes the position he just put himself in."

"I guess you can't fix stupid," Marcus agreed. "Let's hope we have more luck with Dr. Jefferson."

Jefferson's Daniel Island office was located on Clements Ferry Road. The building looked new, and it was clear Dr. Ronald C. Jefferson, M.D. was its only tenant.

The waiting area was empty, aside from an older receptionist behind a sliding glass window.

"Good morning. Can I help you?"

"Yes, ma'am," Adam said and showed the woman his detective shield. "We'd like to speak to Dr. Jefferson, please."

Like most people who are confronted by a detective flashing their badge, she seemed somewhat flustered but managed, "I, um … Dr. Jefferson is with a patient now. Can I tell him what this is about?"

Adam ignored the question. "We'll wait, thank you."

They took seats in the waiting room. It was so quiet that every little movement on the chairs made a rubbery gripping noise—interrupting the *tick tock* of the wall clock.

About ten minutes later, a nicely dressed, middle-aged woman walked out of the examination area, and left after a short conversation with the woman behind the glass window. A moment later, Dr. Jefferson entered the waiting room. "Good morning, gentlemen. Ms. Akerman told me you wanted to see me."

"Yes, sir," Adam said and introduced himself and Marcus.

"We can talk in my office." They followed the doctor to his private office at the end of the hall. Jefferson shut the door and took a seat behind his desk. "I assume this is about Dr. Richardson."

"Yes, sir," Adam replied.

Jefferson took a deep breath. "To be honest, detectives, I'm glad you finally showed up. I'll tell you whatever you need to know. I just want this nightmare to end."

"So you'll tell us about your illegal narcotics distribution?" Adam asked.

"I said I'm willing to talk with you, but you need to understand that I had absolutely nothing to do with what happened to Dr. Richardson or Dr. Bell."

Marcus got right to it. "Dr. Jefferson, I'm sure you're aware that Dr. Charles Richardson was murdered three days ago. We know about your relationship with him and your involvement in the illegal distribution of opioids. Are you admitting that you illegally prescribed and distributed narcotics?" Adam asked.

"I said I'm willing to talk, detectives, but before I say anything, I need my lawyer here."

"Dr. Jefferson," Adam pressed, "you're not being arrested or charged with anything Are you sure you want a lawyer involved?"

"Yes, I'm sure." He walked to the door and called out to his assistant, "Mary, I need you to cancel my afternoon appointments, and please get Sarah Abernathy on the line."

A moment later his phone rang. "Good morning, Sarah, the detectives are here." He hung up and smiled. "She'll be here in about five minutes. Can I get you folks some coffee or soft drinks?"

Adam and Marcus glanced at each other, stunned by what was transpiring. "No thank you, doctor," Adam said.

"Are you sure. I'm getting myself a cup. This may take a while."

"No, we're good, sir."

Jefferson left his office and returned a few minutes later with his coffee and three bottles of water. "Here's some water just in case you change your mind."

Jefferson continued to smile as an awkward silence fell over the group. Finally, Marcus broke it. "How long have you been practicing, doctor?"

Jefferson pointed to a diploma on the wall behind him. "I graduated from the University of Pittsburgh Med School back in '99. Did my internship and residency at Allegheny Hospital before we moved here in 2002."

He was about to say something else when the door opened and an older woman with a briefcase entered the room. She nodded to Jefferson, walked to Adam and Marcus, and extended her hand. "Detectives, I'm Sarah Abernathy, Ron Jefferson's attorney."

Both detectives stood and introduced themselves.

Jefferson pulled up a chair next to his desk. "Sarah, please have a seat."

She thanked him and directed her next comments to the detectives. "You should know that Dr. Jefferson approached me a few days ago regarding a somewhat difficult situation he finds himself in after the recent death of his colleague, Dr. Charles Richardson. He is willing to help you in your investigation. Our problem is that in doing so, he may expose some questionable activities he has been engaged in over the last several years."

"Excuse me, Ms. Abernathy," Adam said. "We know a fair amount about those questionable activities, and because of this,

his life may now be in jeopardy. In order for our department to help him, he's going to have to admit to what he's done and identify the individuals and organizations that participated in these crimes."

"Dr. Jefferson is fully aware of that, detective. And as I was about to say, he is willing to give you that information. However, we'll need assurances that he will not be prosecuted."

"I'm not sure that's going to happen, counselor," Adam said. "But District Attorney Elaine Stewart will make that decision. I'd be more than happy to get her on the phone right now."

"I'm sure Dr. Jefferson would agree with that."

Adam removed his cell phone and dialed Stewart's office.

A moment later, he had her on the line and explained the situation. "Elaine, I've got you on speaker now and will be recording our conversation."

"That's fine. Good morning to all of you," Stewart said. "And Ms. Abernathy, it's nice to speak with you again. It's been a while."

"Yes, it has. As Detective Stone mentioned, my client has information that would be greatly beneficial to his investigation. However, that information may implicate him as well as other individuals. It could also put his life in danger. Before he is willing to do that, we would like assurances that he will not be prosecuted if his information implicates him in any crimes. We would also expect that he would be protected from possible reprisals from those people or organizations he exposes."

"First off, we appreciate Dr. Jefferson's offer to help in the investigation. As far as your request for protection, I'm sure our police department will do what it can to make that happen. While you know I can't guarantee immunity, I can assure you his cooperation will definitely be considered. Sarah, you've known me long enough to know what that means."

"I assume that will be put in writing."

"Of course."

"Thank you, Elaine. I'm going to recommend my client cooperate fully with you and the police in this matter."

Jefferson looked immensely relieved after the call. He flashed his smile at the detectives and said, "Okay, guys, where do we start?"

"How about telling us how you got involved with Dr. Richardson?"

"Sure. I first met Charles a little over five years ago when he referred a patient to me. After he referred a second patient, he suggested we get together for dinner. We hit it off right away and found that we had a lot of things in common. We both worked out and enjoyed running—we even ran side by side in the Cooper River Bridge Run in consecutive years. We both enjoyed firearms and would meet at the Quick Shot Shooting Range on Highway 17 to practice. It didn't take long before we developed a good working relationship. It was around that time that I'd just paid off my medical school loans, and we'd moved into our new house on Daniel Island. My wife, Judy, and I have twin girls, Casey and Gwen, and we enrolled them in the Bishop England School on the island.

"With the new mortgage and the kid's tuition, money started to become a problem. My specialty is pain management, and that's when Charles first mentioned he had a special source of pain meds and explained how he was able to make a good deal of money selling them through his practice. He told me he had some other doctors he was working with and offered to supply me with the meds and show me how to make additional money. I knew it wasn't completely legal, but to be honest, our debts were getting out of hand, and I finally agreed to do it. After a while, serious money started coming in."

"Exactly what do you mean by 'serious money?'" Marcus asked.

Jefferson looked at Abernathy, and she nodded. "All right. You need to understand that physicians working in pain management are acutely aware of both the benefits and the dangers of opioids. Before I got involved with Charles, I was very careful about prescribing them. I also never sold the medications directly to my patients. I wrote prescriptions my patients could fill at their pharmacies."

"I'm assuming that changed after you began working with Dr. Richardson," Marcus said.

"Yes. The whole idea behind the system was not only to increase the strength and amount of the medication prescribed to my patients but also identify individual patients who would be willing to pay cash for the pills. I knew this was wrong, but I initially justified it by convincing myself I was helping them deal with chronic pain."

"When did you begin recruiting and supplying other doctors?" Marcus asked.

"I guess it was six or seven months after he started supplying me with the pills. We were having dinner one night, and he brought it up—he said I could make even more money by recruiting my own group of doctors. Before I knew it, I had three doctors working for me."

"Did your wife know what you were doing?" Adam asked.

"Not at first. I just told Judy that the practice was doing well. After a year or so, we were able to pay down the mortgage. I got new cars for both of us and even put money down on a condo in Naples, Florida. I didn't think twice about writing a check for the twins' tuition at Clemson. But it became harder and harder to deal with the cash the practice was generating. I kept most of it hidden in the attic until Richardson introduced me to some people who would sell me gold, diamonds, and other valuable things I could store and sell later. Charles suggested I put the stuff I'd bought with the cash in a private storage unit."

"Where's the unit?" Adam asked.

"On Seven Farms Drive right here on the island. For the first four years or so the money blinded me, and then starting last year, things started to fall apart. I finally went to see Charles and told him I couldn't do the thing anymore. I wanted out."

"I'm assuming he didn't take it well," Adam said.

"No, he didn't. He said the people he was getting the pills from knew who I was, and if I tried to quit, they'd come after me and my family."

"How long had you been working with Richardson when your wife discovered what you were doing?" Marcus asked.

"A little over five years. With all the money we were spending and things we were buying, Judy started to get suspicious. About a month ago, she told me she knew something was really wrong, and I finally confessed the whole thing. She told me she'd take the kids and leave me if I didn't stop. I promised I would, and when I heard Charles was murdered, I went straight to Sarah. And then we learned that Nathan Bell was also killed."

"Who was supplying Richardson?" Adam asked.

"I have no idea who they were. Honestly. I never met them. Charles always gave me the pills. That's the same way I handled it with my doctors."

"How about the people you bought the gold and jewelry from?"

"I only dealt with one person, and I never knew his name. Charles set it up the first time we met. I'd give him the cash, and a week or so later he'd give me the stuff and a burner phone. I'd use the phone to call him the next time. That's how it worked."

At this point, it was clear Jefferson was all in. Adam and Marcus spent another hour questioning him. Like Richardson, he had kept track of the numbers. Jefferson provided names and addresses of the doctors he supplied, and a list of the patients who bought his OXY. He also gave them the key for his storage unit and written permission for the police to confiscate the contents inside. In addition, he gave formal authorization to search his home and office and take all computers and phones.

As the interrogation was coming to an end, Adam told Jefferson the department has arranged to have a police officer watch his home between 6:00 p.m. and 6:00 a.m.

"I didn't see anyone there last night," Jefferson replied.

"I'm sure he was there. Our officers are trained to stake out a location without it being obvious. Our captain issued the surveillance order yesterday morning. You mentioned your daughters. Are they still at school?"

"They are, until Thanksgiving break."

"Good. Do you or your wife have relatives in the area?"

"Judy's sister and her husband live in Columbia."

"I suggest your wife stay with them until this is over."

"I'm sure that won't be a problem. What should I do?"

"It's important you continue to see patients as you normally would," Adam answered. "Again, we'll have officers shadowing you."

"It sounds like I'm the bait for whoever killed Charles and Dr. Bell."

"You're not bait," Adam said, "but you're almost certainly a target. And there's no doubt you'll be safer if a police officer is with you."

Abernathy broke in. "I just want to emphasize that the safety of my client and his family needs to be paramount in this arrangement."

"Understood," Adam replied. "We'll stay in contact as this plays out."

Adam and Marcus stood—the meeting was over.

CHAPTER TEN

ADAM AND MARCUS took Jefferson with them to Stockade Storage on Seven Farms Drive. The attendant buzzed them on through, and they pulled up in front of unit #110.

"This should be interesting," Marcus said as they watched Jefferson unlock the unit and pull up the garage door.

"Holy shit!" Adam said.

The unit was ten feet square with floor to ceiling wooden shelves built against the back wall. Several rolled up oriental rugs were pushed against the right wall next to a long table that held ten to fifteen large oil paintings. A futuristic-looking LOTUS C-01 black motorcycle was parked against the left wall.

Adam was admiring the motorcycle when Marcus said, "Adam, look at this!" He stood slack-jawed in front of a box filled with jewelry, cut diamonds, and Rolex watches.

A good-sized safe sat on a shelf. "I bet that's where he kept his cash and maybe the OXY," Marcus commented.

"I've got no idea how much all this stuff is worth," Adam said, "but it's got to be a shitload. And we don't know what's in the safe."

"Those watches alone are worth a ton," Marcus said. "This stuff won't help us catch our Mr. Sandman, but It's a hell of a haul for the department."

Adam took pictures of the items in Jefferson's unit.

They left Stockade Storage and dropped Jefferson off back at his office before leaving to check the storage facilities around Dr. Richardson's PRO Care office. Adam reassured Dr. Jefferson that an officer would be back out at his home that evening.

They hit paydirt when the key opened the lock on unit #128 at the third facility they visited. It was a CubeSmart Self Storage on Rivers Avenue and took a good deal of self-control for the detectives not to look inside. But, as agreed, they would have to cool their heels until Judge Roberts issued the warrant. They waited over an hour at the courthouse until the judge had a short recess in a trial and approved the warrant.

They returned to the Rivers Avenue facility warrant in hand, and after seeing Jefferson's cache, they were even more amazed at what Richardson's unit held. Like Jefferson's, it contained a variety of artwork, jewelry, gold, and diamonds, but there were also metal boxes containing bundles of cash. What surprised them most was the shiny dark silver Porsche 918 Spyder. A half-hour was spent scrutinizing and taking pictures of the contents before sealing the door and leaving for the Lockwood station.

They reported their findings and gave forensics the storage keys to both storage units before returning to their desks to write their report and update the murder books.

~~~~

It was after 7:00 in the evening when Marcus suggested they call Walczak in Chicago to see what he knows about Eddie Santoro's part in moving the Chinese oxycodone and this Sandman character.

Adam made the call and the former chief answered with a curt "Walczak."

"Chief, this is detective Adam Stone from Charleston, South Carolina. I'm here with …"

"You at the station?"

"Yes, sir."

"I'll call you back."

A few moments later, the desk sergeant patched Walczak's call through.

"Sorry about that, boys. Can't be too careful. Now what is it you need?"

Adam put the phone on speaker and offered the bullet points of the two homicides that involved the illegal distribution of oxycodone while Walczak breathed into the phone. They could hear Walczak's stubble scratching against the mouthpiece.
~~~~

"What can you tell us about that?" Adam asked.

"I've been retired for a time now, but my friends keep me in the loop. First off, your information is good, but it's not just Eddie Santoro running the pill business. The whole Chicago Organization is into it, and it's being directed by DeLaurentis and his underboss, Emilio Cataudella. We know they're getting their product from China—we're just not sure how they're bringing it in. And it's not just OXY. China's a big supplier of fentanyl, and we're seeing more and more of that on the street. What's worst is that some of the OXY is being laced with fentanyl, and our OD deaths are way up."

"Chief, this is Detective Williams. It sounds like Charleston's not the only place getting hit with the stuff out of Chicago. How widespread is it?"

"They're moving their product throughout several major cities in the Midwest and South. We've been working with the FBI and DEA on it."

"Our department is also working with the FBI," Adam added, "but most of their resources are directed toward heroin and crack cocaine."

"There's another thing we wanted to talk to you about," Marcus said. "The murders we're investigating look like professional hits. One of our undercovers heard talk about an old hitman out of Chicago called the Sandman."

There was no response. Marcus began to repeat himself when Walczak cut him off.

"I heard you. Who told your guy about the Sandman?"

"One of Nick Santoro's people," Adam said. "Apparently, the guy was drunk and let it slip."

"All right, here's what I can tell you," Walczak began. "As you know, there were hundreds of mob-related murders in Chicago back in the 70s and 80s. I remember it was like the Wild West. The story goes that in the early 90s, the Outfit's boss, Tony Accardo, sent Tommy 'The Ant' Spilotro and his brother, Michael, out to Vegas to supervise the mob's casinos. Tommy Spilotro developed a reputation for fast cars, fast women, and a loose tongue.

"Eventually, the Outfit grew tired of Tommy's wild ways, and Accardo gave the order to eliminate him. Word was that after a night of drinking and carousing, the Spilotro brothers and two women returned to their suite in the Flamingo. The next morning, they were found dead in their room—both brothers and the women shot several times in the chest and once each in the head. What was strange about the whole thing was that the four bodies were left lined up in a row like, their arms crossed over their chests like they were sleeping. Each of them had a small amount of sand on their faces. That's where this hitman Accardo used got the name, Sandman. And from then on it appeared that this Sandman guy only worked for Accardo and only on the mob's high profile murders. Word started to spread that the Sandman was some kind of psycho— like he needed to kill, and if the mob hadn't swooped him up he'd have become a serial killer or something.

"Apparently, Accardo was the only person who knew the real identity of this Sandman. There were some twenty-two murders between 1992 and 2014 where the Sandman left his calling card. There's a chance some of these were copycat killings, but none was ever solved. In 2014, Accardo passed on the leadership of the Chicago Outfit to Salvatore DeLaurentis—and with it the identity of the Sandman."

"Have there been any mob killings since 2014 that match the way the Sandman leaves his victims?" Marcus asked.

"Nothing until last month—then three showed up—one in Cleveland, one in St. Louis, and one in Memphis. There have been rumblings lately that Chicago is trying to eliminate the distribution channels for pills coming in from Mexico."

"That would explain the murder of the two doctors we're investigating," Adam acknowledged.

"Could be but remember all this is just rumor and innuendo. But if it is true, and the Sandman is in Charleston—then you've got a major problem on your hands."

"That's what we're worried about," Adam said. "We appreciate everything you've told us, sir. We'll keep you appraised of what develops, and please let us know if you hear anything else."

"Will do, my friends. Give my best to Chief Taylor and be safe."

Adam hung up and Marcus said, "Looks like Charleston isn't the only place Chicago is sending the message about Mexican pills."

"Right," Adam replied, "and we need to up our protection for doctors Morgan and Jefferson."

Marcus was about to say something when they heard Boyer call out, "Where are you two going?"

"Back to our desks," Marcus said over his shoulder.

Adam was alongside him but stopped to ask which officers Boyer had sent to shadow Morgan and Jefferson.

"I thought you were doing that," Boyer answered.

"No, Captain. You said you'd take care of it. Jesus, Frank, are you saying nobody's been watching those doctors?"

Boyer's face turned the color of a bright red tomato. "I said I thought you were going to do it."

Marcus turned on his heels and leveled a nasty gaze on Boyer. "Wait a second. How about our families? Did you assign Rodriguez and Fitzgerald to stay with them?"

"No, I thought you said Merchant did that."

"God damn it, Frank," Adam said. "We told you Merchant wanted you to do that. You're the captain!"

"All right, all right," Boyer replied, his embarrassment clearly showing. "Take it easy. I'll take care of it now. I'll assign Cummings and Winthrop to Morgan and Salazar can sit on Jefferson."

"Get the damn things done this time!" Adam said, his anger mounting.

"You better watch your tone, detective."

Adam took a step toward Boyer, but Marcus grabbed his arm and said, "We're talking about our families. Just make sure you get both those things done, Captain."

Boyer turned and walked back to his office—no doubt thinking of ways to blame someone else for his mistake.

"That son of a bitch," Adam mumbled. He looked at his watch and called Tracy to let her know an officer would be there shortly. Marcus also called Makayla to advise her.

~~~~

Back at their desks, Marcus suggested they take a moment to go over where they were on the investigation.

"Good idea," Adam said. "A lot of shit has happened over the past few days, but we're still spinning our wheels on coming much closer to finding the killer—even if it's this Sandman guy."

"Right," Marcus replied. "It's becoming clear that Chicago sanctioned the hit, and Nick Santoro has to have known it was going down. Morgan and Jefferson are still in danger, but hopefully, we'll be ready if whoever killed Richardson and Bell decides to make a move on either of them."

Adam agreed. "We know drugs are the reason for the killings, and Chicago is at the center of changes in the drug business in Charleston. Our focus has to remain on the killer—whoever that might be. I'm also concerned about what Lucas Vicario might try to do to our families. But I do feel better now that Rodriguez and Fitzgerald will be with them when we're not there."

"I agree with all of that, brother. I'm also thinking we need to check and make sure Boyer followed through on assigning the officers at our two doctors' houses."
~~~~

Adam and Marcus went back to Boyer's office to make sure he'd followed up—only to find that he'd left for the day.

Marcus asked his assistant about the arrangements for the officers to cover their homes and those of the two doctors.

"He told me to let you know that he took care of both of your problems," the assistant responded.

Adam looked at Marcus and shook his head. "So, now they're our problems."

"Who'd he assign to shadow the doctors?" Marcus asked.

"Hang on a second." She rummaged through some papers on her desk until she picked up one. "Here it is. In addition to Officers Fitzgerald and Rodriguez at your places, he's assigned Officer Cummings at Dr. Morgan's house, and Officer Salazar will be with Dr. Jefferson."

"Wait a second," Adam said. "What about Officer Winthrop? He was supposed to be assigned with Cummings to watch Dr. Morgan's place."

"I don't know anything about that. Frank only told me Cummings was to cover Dr. Morgan."

"We told Frank that Dr. Morgan doesn't know we'll be watching his place. We need two officers to cover it effectively."

"There's not much we can do about it now," Marcus said and asked Boyer's assistant to try to get ahold of Officer Winthrop and request he join Cummings at Morgan's townhouse.

Adam left lamenting, "What a jackass!"

"I think it's a good bet Boyer never passed on all the information you gave him on each of the doctors," Marcus said. "We should probably stop by their houses and make sure Cummings and Salazar are up to speed on everything."

"Good idea," Adam agreed. "I've got copies of the information Boyer was supposed to give to the officers. I'll meet Officer Salazar at Jefferson's house, and you can check out Cummings at Morgan's place? It's already 9:00, and after we finish with that, there's not much more we can do tonight. We've been working four straight days with little to no sleep, and we're both running on empty. I say when we're done checking on the officers, we go home, see the family, and grab a few hours of sleep before coming back here."

The detectives drove to the house of their respective doctor and spent an hour or so with the officer assigned to each. Once they were comfortable that their officer was properly prepared to deal with the situation, they headed home for a quick nap before they'd return to the station early the next morning.

CHAPTER ELEVEN

ARRIVING HOME LATER that evening, Marcus was pleased to see Officer Rodriguez parked outside and told him to take the rest of the night off but to make sure he was back at 6:00 sharp. Makayla was waiting inside with a bottle of wine, and the two spent a quiet and well-deserved evening together.

At 5:00 the next morning, Marcus was up and feeling refreshed. He took a shower and ate a light breakfast. When Officer Rodriguez arrived at 6:00, Marcus kissed Makayla goodbye, and left for the station. He was backing out of the garage when his headlights illuminated the front of his house. He slammed on the brakes, clinched his teeth, and seethed, "God damn it!"

He jumped out and flung the door shut. His eyes were riveted on the front of his house—10-105 and 10-82 had been spray-painted in black paint. He took several pictures with his phone then went inside with Rodriguez to tell Makayla what happened. He checked the visuals on his security camera but could not identify the culprit who had his face covered by a ski mask.

Rodriguez remained with Makayla, and Marcus left fuming for Lockwood.

Adam was already at his desk, and after Marcus told him what had happened the night before, they both went directly to Chief Merchant's office. The chief agreed that from now on, Officer Rodriguez would not only shadow Makayla during the daytime but spend the entire night inside their home. The same arrangements were made for Officer Fitzgerald to protect Piper and Tracy. Once Merchant completed updating the assignments, he asked if the detectives needed any other resources on the Richardson and Bell murders.

"I think we're good," Adam answered. "Gagyi is working the computers and cell phones forensics confiscated. Tonight we've got Salazar on the Jefferson home. Dr. Morgan refused to cooperate, but we've arranged to have Officer Cummings cover his residence. Morgan's not aware we'll be watching him. We're hoping we can get Boyer to shake loose Officer Winthrop to help Cummings cover Morgan's place. Now it's a waiting game to see if any moves are made on Morgan or Jefferson."

Back at the bullpen, a package had been delivered from Mt. Pleasant with the initial results from the search of Bell's home and office. Like Richardson, Bell had a stable of doctors buying OXY from him, but he seemed to be operating on a much smaller scale.

Adam and Marcus prepared warrants and affidavits for Morgan's home and office but were surprised and disappointed when Judge Roberts balked at issuing the warrants. He ruled that without written documentation or direct evidence that Morgan had actually purchased oxycodone from Richardson, the warrant didn't have probable cause.

Despite this, the detectives felt they now had a good sense of why the two doctors were murdered and that both Chicago and Nick Santoro were behind it. Catching the murderer was another matter, but with the officers assigned to protect Morgan and Jefferson, they were confident they'd be ready should this mysterious Sandman make a move on them. During a break, Marcus suggested they bring in Richardson's assistant for further questioning. "I don't think there's any question she knew Richardson was pushing OXY. It's a longshot, but maybe she can link one of their patients to Santoro's people."

"True," Adam replied. "Plus, it's hard to believe she didn't know any of those fifteen direct clients Richardson was supplying."

Adam called Novak and assured her it was just a simple follow-up meeting and nothing for her to worry about. She reluctantly agreed to come down to the station. Marcus escorted her to the small conference room Gagyi had been using to research the confiscated computers and cell phones.

"Thanks again, Ms. Novak," Adam began. "We appreciate your help on this."

Adam had a printout of the names of Dr. Richardson's fifteen direct clients. "We'd like you to take another look at these names. Take your time and let us know if you recognize any of them."

She took only a cursory look before answering, "No, I can't say I do. I'm pretty sure none of them were our patients."

"So, you don't recognize a single name?" Adam asked.

"I'm sure," Novak answered a bit too quickly.

"All right. Do you recall anything that happened over the last month or two that seemed unusual? Perhaps a patient or visitor who did something out of the ordinary."

"No, not really." Again, her answer came with a bit too much haste.

Adam leaned forward. "Ms. Novak, we're going to be perfectly honest with you. We have evidence Dr. Richardson was involved in the illegal distribution of opioids, and this undoubtedly led to his murder. We also believe you may have been complicit in what he did. We are willing to help you, but only if you're totally honest with us."

Novak was obviously nervous. Ever since Richardson's murder, she knew that her life might be in danger. She felt trapped but could only manage to say, "I didn't really think he was doing anything wrong."

"I'm going to give you one more chance," Adam said. "I suggest you think hard before you answer this time. Do you remember anything out of the ordinary that happened at the office over the last few months?"

This time she took longer before answering. "Okay, there was something. It was about a month or so ago. I was closing the office one day after work when this man showed up. I told him we were closed, but he said he needed to see Charles and pushed the door open. He went right into his office and closed the door. He was only in there a few minutes before he left. And he came back the next day about the same time."

"Could you hear what they were talking about?" Adam asked. "Anything at all?"

"Not really. I just remember Charles shouted something about a 'shantono' or something like that."

"Santoro?" Adam quickly asked. "Did he say Santoro?"

"Maybe, I can't remember exactly."

Adam shot a look at Marcus and their eyes locked. "I'll get the book," Marcus said.

He was back in the conference room a few minutes later carrying a large three-ring binder. Adam took the binder, opened it, and placed it in front of Novak.

"Ms. Novak, I want you to go through these pictures and tell me if perhaps you see the man you just mentioned. No rush now. Please, take your time."

She began flipping through the book slowly with her forehead scrunched. Finally, she pointed to a picture and said, "This is the man. I'm sure of it."

Susan Novak had just identified Liam Burns—known to be a bodyguard for Nick Santoro.

Novak was now becoming more and more nervous. Eyes downcast, she felt flush, and her breathing accelerated. "What's going to happen to me?"

"Nothing for the time being," Adam said. "If you continue to cooperate with us, I'm sure we can work something out. You've been helpful—let's make sure it stays that way."

"I'll do whatever you want. I promise."

Adam walked Novak out of the conference room, and when he returned, Marcus wasn't smiling. "All right, so now we got a direct link between Dr. Richardson and Nick Santoro. But let's face it, partner, we've still got no hard evidence who ordered the murder or who actually did it. We're spinning our wheels here. Everything points to the Chicago Outfit, but all we've got is that one of Nick Santoro's boys met with Richardson and a story about some old ghost hitman called the Sandman. It's so damn frustrating!"

~~~~

One of Chief Merchant's assistants stuck his head in the conference room and told them they were wanted in his office. When they got there, Chito Walker, the SWAT Team commander, was seated outside. They acknowledged Walker and entered Merchant's office where they found their local FBI agent, James Franco, Frank Boyer, and another man.
~~~~

The chief told them to take a seat and gestured to the third man. "Detectives, this is Special Agent Ben Bradford. Ben, meet Detectives Adam Stone and Marcus Williams."

They shook hands and Merchant continued, "Agent Bradford is with Chicago's FBI field office and will be working with Agent Franco and us on the opioid distribution here in Charleston. He's part of a special FBI task force investigating Chinese oxycodone in Chicago. I've briefed him on the Richardson and Bell murders. Ben, go ahead and tell the detectives what you've got."

"Thank you, Chief. About a year and a half ago, we first noticed an increased presence of Chinese-made oxycodone pills on the streets of Chicago and its suburbs. Prior to this, well over 90% of these illegal pills originated in Mexico. But since then, we've seen a steady decline in the Mexican product and an increase in the Chinese product in the Chicago market. We also know the Chicago Mafia is importing the Chinese product and distributing it to several cities throughout the Midwest and South."

Merchant added that Agent Bradford was aware of Nick Santoro's effort to eliminate the local suppliers of Mexican-made OXY.

"Correct," Bradford affirmed. "We're in the final stages of an operation to eliminate, or at least, disrupt, the Outfit's distribution channels. To be more specific, we've identified local organizations involved in distributing the Chinese product in our target cities—one of which is Nick Santoro's organization here in Charleston. Agent Franco will be working with your department on what we are calling, 'Operation Blackout.' James will take it from here."

"Thank you, Ben. Operation Blackout will target Charleston and eight other cities where we've identified major dealers of the Chinese product. We plan to utilize local law enforcement along with FBI and DEA agents and initiate the operation simultaneously in all nine target cities. With today's meeting, Special Agent Bradford has now met with local law enforcement in all nine cities. Sorry you're just hearing about this, but we wanted to keep the operation under the radar for as long as possible." Agent Franco nodded to Merchant indicating he was finished.

"Thank you, Agent Franco." Merchant stood. "That will be all for today. I know Agent Bradford needs to get back to Chicago. Agent Franco will keep us updated on the progress and timing of the operation."

Bradford and Franco got up and left. Merchant asked the remainder of the men to stay seated and brought Chito Walker into the room. "All right, gentlemen, there's another matter we need to deal with—the graffiti spray-painted on the detectives' homes. We're confident this was ordered by Lucas Vicario in an effort to reestablish the Posse's reputation, which we know was seriously damaged after Spider Gomez's death and the loss of the Sinaloa Cartel's heroin business."

Adam interrupted, "Listen, Chief, Marcus and I appreciate you assigning officers to watch our families, but that doesn't solve the problem."

"Stone, if you'd sit there and be quiet for a minute, I'll finish what I was trying to say."

"Yes, sir. Sorry."

"Okay, then. Blackwood has picked up intel from his contacts that some tension is building within the upper ranks of the Posse. Vicario has ordered his boys to move in on a few of the Bloods' dealers and has even started to hassle some of our street officers. His attempts to reestablish the Posse's cred is being questioned by his next-in-line lieutenant, Angel Rivera. Rivera believes Vicario's actions will only push the police to react and further weaken their position rather than strengthen it."

"I say we hit Vicario and this Angel Rivera hard," Boyer said. "Let's bring in some of his crew. Get some search warrants. Give them a taste of their own medicine."

"That's an option, Frank," Merchant said. "But Terry made another suggestion, and I tend to agree with him. First, we make it known that the department's main priority was dealing with Santoro and the Bloods, and that we were not overly concerned with the Posse. But the attacks on Williams and Stone have changed all that. Now the department is coming for the Posse and its businesses."

"Do you think that's enough to shift power from Vicario to Rivera?" Marcus asked.

"No, probably not. Terry suggested we have our SWAT Team make a few targeted hits on their assets. Nothing too serious, just enough to plant doubt about Vicario's leadership. We'll have our informants drop hints that the increased pressure was due directly to Vicario's decisions. Terry thinks it might be enough to get Rivera and his followers to move against Vicario. If we can get him out of the picture, the pressure on Adam and Marcus' families should ease up."

"It may work," Marcus said. "But if it doesn't, you got to figure Vicario will become even more emboldened."

"That's always a possibility," Merchant acknowledged. "That's why I wanted some feedback, especially from you and Adam."

"I say we hit them hard," Boyer said. "Take off the gloves and let them know we mean business."

"Marcus, your thoughts?" asked Merchant, all but ignoring Boyer.

"There's definitely a risk, but if we plant some doubt beforehand, and don't go overboard with SWAT, I think it might work."

"Adam?"

"I'm with Marcus."

"Okay," Merchant said. "Chito, is this something you can do effectively?"

"I see no problem, sir."

"All right, I want the three of you to get with Chito. When you have a plan, I'll take a look at it and run it by Blackwood. In the meantime, continue to gather intel on Nick Santoro and his OXY distribution network without tipping off his people. We'll need that for Operation Blackout. Now, get to work."

CHAPTER TWELVE

EARLIER THAT EVENING, Dr. Sam Morgan and his assistant, Martha Simpson, were downtown at the Pavilion Bar on East Bay.

Simpson had just ordered her third scotch when she said, "I'm worried, Sam. What's going to happen to me if those detectives find out about everything you've been doing?"

Morgan frowned. "*I've* been doing! You're in this thing as much as I am. So just calm down. As long as you destroyed all those records like I told you to, they've got nothing. We've had a good run, but I think it's time to take what we've got and head out west."

"If we're going to do that, we better do it quick." Simpson lowered her voice to a whisper. "Look what happened to Richardson and Bell. I'm more worried about that than anything."

"Listen, I've already talked to people I know in Portland. I can close the office and list the building and my condo with my real estate agent. It'll only take a few days to make the arrangements, and we can be out of here in a week or so. It may take a while for me to get licensed in Oregon, but I've got plenty of cash for us to get established out there."

"The sooner the better," Martha said.

Morgan glanced at his watch. "Let's get out of here. I've got a golf game first thing in the morning."

They finished their drinks, left the bar, and arrived back at Morgan's James Island townhouse—completely unaware of the unmarked police car parked across from his building. Officer Brandon Cummings noted the time of their return.

Martha turned off a few lights and flashed a seductive smile. "Sam, get me a scotch," she said. "I'll slip into something more comfortable."

"All right, but I'm going to bed. The guys are picking me up at 6:00 in the morning."

Simpson felt rejected and stewed for a while before eventually joining Morgan in bed, and they both slept soundly.

The night was still until 4:00 a.m.

A figure shrouded in darkness pulled his pale-gray hooded sweatshirt over his head and moved surreptitiously from a patch of woods behind the row of townhouses. With the stealth of a serpent, he crept up the wooden stairs to the rear deck of the townhouse. Less than thirty seconds later, the lock was picked, and the man quietly stepped through the sliding glass door. The moonlight cast enough light for the man to navigate his way through the living room and down the hallway to the master bedroom. He entered the bedroom and moved slowly to the bed where the naked bodies of Sam Morgan and Martha Simpson lay partially covered by white silk sheets.

The man took in his surroundings before raising his Beretta 71 with an attached rimfire suppressor and fired two .22LR caliber bullets into the chest and a third into the center of Sam Morgan's forehead. Before she had a chance to react, he shifted the gun toward the woman lying next to him and shot her.

The man lowered his gun and gently positioned the bodies on their backs—arms folded over their chest. He remained in the bedroom for some time admiring the dead man and woman. Eventually, he stood, reached into his pocket, and removed a small amount of sand. He sprinkled the sand over the two dead bodies, backed out of the bedroom, and disappeared into the night.

<div align="center">~~~~</div>

A few hours later, morning slipped through the bedroom window bathing the room in soft slate-gray light.

Officer Brandon Cummings had spent a long, tiring, uneventful night confined in his unmarked police car surveilling Sam Morgan's townhouse. He'd just slipped out of the car to have another cigarette when he saw a silver BMW carrying three men pull up in front of Morgan's townhouse. A man dressed in golf attire exited the car and jogged up the stairs to Morgan's front door. He knocked several times. No response.

He waited a moment and knocked again—still no response. He turned back toward the BMW—frustration painted across his face. He jogged back down the stairs and disappeared around the side of the building.

Up the stairs to the rear deck, he noticed the sliding glass door was partially open. He called out Morgan's name and still getting no response entered the townhouse and made his way down the hall to the bedroom.

He froze—his mind trying to process the grisly scene that lay in front of him. Morgan and a woman lying next to him were covered in blood—the dark red in stark contrast to the white sheets that partially covered them. He almost fell as he stumbled out of the bedroom and down the back stairs.

Officer Cummings saw the man racing around the building and muttered to himself, "Holy shit!" He dropped his cigarette, pulled out his Glock, and intercepted the man halfway across the parking lot.

Holding up his badge in his left hand, he yelled, "Police! What's happening?"

"Jesus! They're both dead!"

Cummings activated his shoulder radio. "Lockwood! It's Officer Cummings! I've got a situation! Need backup. Now! I repeat—I've got a 10-43. Harborwalk condos on Nabors Drive. Need backup now!"

By now, the other two men were out of the BMW. Cummings ordered them to stay where they were, and got the man calmed down enough to describe what he'd witnessed in more detail.

It felt like forever before two squad cars finally arrived. The two officers joined Cummings who gave them a quick account of the situation. Cummings directed one officer to cover the front door while he and the other officer proceeded to the rear of the building and entered the townhouse.

They made their way to the bedroom where they found Morgan and Simpson covered in a sea of blood.

~~~~

When they arrived at the scene, Marcus told Adam to go ahead and check out the townhouse, and he'll talk to Cummings.

They both grabbed a pair of gloves and booties before leaving the Charger. Adam motioned one of the other officers to follow him. Marcus approached Cummings—his anger palpable. "What the hell happened!"

"I don't know, sir. I've been here since 6:00 yesterday evening, and nobody other than Morgan and Simpson went in or out of the townhouse last night. I swear I never left my post, sir."

"Where the hell is Winthrop?"

"I don't know, sir."

Marcus shook his head and looked toward the three men standing by the BMW being interview by officers. "When did they get here?"

Cummings related details from when the BMW arrived around 6:00 to when he found the dead bodies. "I'm really sorry, sir."
~~~~

"I want your report on my desk this morning," Marcus ordered.

Marcus jogged up the rear stairs and entered the town-house. A half-empty glass of brown liquor rested on the coffee table. A suit jacket was draped over the back of a chair and two high heels shoes lay haphazard on the floor. He entered the bedroom careful not to touch anything. Morgan and Simpson were lying in the bed next to each other—their arms crossed as if in sleep. The bed was steeped in blood, and the bloodstained bedsheet half-on, half-off the bed.

"Jesus Christ," he muttered.

"Yeah. What did you get out of Cummings?" Adam asked.

"Nothing really. Swears he watched the place all night. Morgan and Simpson got back around 9:00 last night. No one else went in or out until he called it in."

"Well, it looks like someone did," Adam said and pointed to the bodies. "Take a closer look."

Marcus stepped around the blood that had pooled on the floor at the base of the bed. He put his hands on his knees and bent down. He straightened up, glanced at Adam, and said, "Sand."

"Exactly. Looks like our Sandman paid a visit last night."

A few minutes later, they heard the front door open, and three forensic techs appeared at the bedroom door. Adam briefly explained what little they knew. He was about to leave when he noticed the sliding glass door leading to the rear deck partially opened and told the techs to dust for prints and determine whether the lock had been picked.

The detectives went outside and walked around the building. They found a small creek and a narrow row of trees behind the townhouses, cover the killer likely used to access the scene. He couldn't believe it was that easy to get around their surveillance. He immediately realized the mistake of not having the second officer stationed behind the building.

Adam told the techs to check the wooded area for footprints then suggested Marcus remain at the scene while he pushed forward on procedural matters. "O'Sullivan should be here soon," he said. "I'll get back, bring Boyer and Merchant up to speed, and get started on a warrant for Morgan's office. Judge Roberts will sure as hell approve it this time."

~~~~

It was about noon by the time Adam had the warrant and affidavit written and signed off by the judge. He'd just returned to the bullpen when he heard Boyer call out, "Stone, get in here!"

He shut his eyes, took a deep breath, and walked over to Boyer.

"Where's Williams?"

"Still at the crime scene."

"Who screwed up the surveillance?"

"Frank, *you* were supposed to assign Winthrop. You didn't and that only left Cummings to cover the whole place. Damn it, Frank, I told you that … oh, hell, just forget it. Marcus should be back shortly. He'll update you."

"Just tell Williams I want to see him"
~~~~

Adam saw no upside in pushing back and left for his desk.

Marcus returned a half-hour later and gave Adam an update. "Forensics found scratches on the sliding door lock. No casings, just like the Richardson and Bell murders. At face, nothing looks to have been stolen. Techs lifted prints from the sliding glass door, the glasses on the coffee table, door jams leading to the master bedroom, some other spots. You got to figure the killer wore gloves."

"What did O'Sullivan have to say?"

"No slugs were found, but she's sure they're inside the bodies. She'll start the autopsy later today. Like the Richardson and Bell crime scenes, there wasn't much blood from the headshot. The massive blood loss came from the shots to the chest. I was leaving and she said to tell you, 'Three's a charm'—as in the same person committed all the murders."

"No argument there."

"Did you get the warrant for Morgan's office?"

"I did," Adam answered. "To be honest, I'm not sure it'll be much help though. We know Morgan was doing the same thing Richardson and Bell were doing with the OXY. It's obvious everything we've found points to this mysterious Sandman."

"You're right. But we still don't know who the guy is—much less who actually ordered the hit."

~~~~
~~~~

Frustrated that nothing much new was learned from the Morgan and Simpson murders that would help in the murder investigations, the detectives returned to their desks—only to find a handwritten note: *See Boyer.*

"I'm not in the mood for this shit," Adam said through clenched teeth.

"I hear you, partner. Let's just go and get whatever the hell he wants over with."

But Boyer wasn't in his office. Marcus asked his assistant the reason for the meeting.

"He mentioned something about Lucas Vicario."

"Where is he?" Adam asked.

"Sorry, guys. He left about a half-hour ago. Didn't say where he was going."

"All right," Marcus said, "just tell him we stopped by."

On the way back to their desks, Adam said, "Doesn't look like we'll get anything from O'Sullivan or forensics for a while. I say we go ahead and handle the Vicario thing ourselves. Actually, I'd rather do it without Frank."

Marcus agreed. "Let's head over to Chito's office and get started on Vicario."

It took an hour to craft a comprehensive plan that targeted Vicario's shot-calling capabilities. It was now time to bring in Jimmy Moreno and make it clear the department knew the hit on Adam's apartment came directly from Vicario. The plan also outlined ways officers could interrupt the Posse's gambling, prostitution, and drug dealing operations. In addition, the plan identified when and where Chito and his SWAT Team would carry out targeted raids—all in an effort to convince Angel Rivera and his boys to force out Vicario.

They caught Chief Merchant before he left for the day and presented their plan. Merchant liked the proposal, made a few tweaks, then told them to advise Boyer that he wanted the plan initiated immediately.

~~~~

Adam and Marcus headed down to forensics to check on what had been discovered at Morgan's townhouse. CSI was still analyzing the items taken from the Morgan crime scene, and Gagyi had only just begun deciphering the contents of both Morgan's computer and cell phone—as well as Martha Simpson's cell. Two large bottles of oxycodone whose labels were written in Spanish and $9,800 in cash were found in Morgan's closet. As expected, the fingerprints lifted lent little to the investigation—the killer had obviously worn gloves.

The techs did find fresh shoe prints by the creek behind the townhouses. They were identified as size 12.5 Nike Air Max 200. Security cameras showed a figure on the grounds around 4:00 a.m. The face was covered by a dark hooded sweatshirt, but it looked to be a man with a slight limp. Forensics estimated the killer's height to be roughly 6' 4". This was based on security camera footage and the trajectory of the bullets entering the victim's head and chest.

Marcus suggested Adam go to Dr. Jefferson's residence, meet Officer Salazar, and check to make sure the house was secure.
~~~~

He would remain at the station initiate the Morgan/Simpson murder book and monitor CSI's progress.

~~~~

Jefferson's house was impressive to say the least. It sat at the end of a cul-de-sac and backed up to the Wando River. The lawn was well attended with a variety of colorful flowering bushes complementing the raised front porch. The walkway was made of Taverna pavers. An expansive second floor deck was supported by a series of large Doric white columns. There was a swimming pool in the backyard and a good-sized gazebo surrounded by Windmill palms overlooking the river.

Officer Dennis Salazar answered the door and told Adam that Dr. Jefferson had been holed up in his study.

"The guy is really depressed. I tried to get him to eat something, but he refused. He's convinced some dude's about to come in here and cap him in the back of the head."

"All right, I'll talk with him, but I first want to check the house to make sure it's as secure as possible."

"I checked already," Salazar said, "but it won't hurt to take another look. The house has a good security setup. Cameras cover the grounds and all the entrances. The whole house can be monitored from Jefferson's cell phone and computer. Dr. Jefferson gave me the login and password for the system, and I've already downloaded the app onto my phone." Salazar took a minute to load the security program onto Adam's phone.
~~~~

After Salazar guided him through the house, Adam felt comfortable that Jefferson was well protected.

"Thanks, Dennis. I'm going to go check on Dr. Jefferson." Before he left, he noticed that Salazar looked pale and his eyes were red and swollen. "Salazar, are you okay? You don't look so good."

"Just feeling a little punk, sir. My wife has the flu, and I might have a touch of it myself. I'll be okay."

The study was on the first floor in the rear of the house. Adam knocked.

"Dr. Jefferson, it's Detective Stone. May I come in?" There was no answer. Adam waited a moment and then eased the door open to find Jefferson seated in one of two leather chairs facing a large fireplace. He didn't acknowledge Adam.

"Excuse me, sir. Can we talk?"

Eyes still focused on the empty fireplace, Jefferson simply said, "Come in, detective." Jefferson lifted a cut-crystal tumbler filled with amber-colored liquid. "There's a bar over there. Gets yourself a drink."

"I'm good, thank you," Adam replied. "How are you holding up, sir?"

Jefferson turned and looked at Adam. His hair was disheveled and dark circles could be seen under his eyes—his pain evident. "How do you think I'm holding up, detective? Richardson, Bell, and Morgan are dead. Who do you think is next on the list?"

"I understand, sir. But your security system is top notch, and we'll be monitoring it 24/7. Officer Salazar will be with you from now on. He's an excellent officer."

Jefferson turned away from Adam and gazed out his window. He was quiet for some time before saying, "I never wanted to be anything other than a doctor—ever since I was a kid. All those years of hard work, years of helping people thrown away because I thought money would solve my problems. I forgot what's really important, and now my family's going to pay for what I've done."

"All that may be true," Adam said, "but what we need to do now is make sure you and your family stay as safe as possible."

"Let's hope so—at least for Judy and the kids' sake." Jefferson put down his drink and asked, "Do you really think this killer is coming after me?"

"It's possible. But, like I said, you've got a good security system, and Officer Salazar will be with you at all times. Listen to him, do what he says, and you should be okay."

Jefferson again seemed lost in his thoughts. "I just want to make sure my wife and girls are going to be safe."

"I understand perfectly, sir. But we'll be monitoring everything. Officer Salazar will be here with you all night. I need to get back to the station, but you can call me if you've got any questions."

"Thank you, detective."

On his way out, Adam stopped to talk to Officer Salazar. "Keep your eye on Jefferson. He's not doing so well. Speaking of not doing well, how about you? You look like you're about to pass out."

"Don't worry about me, sir. I'll be fine."

~~~~

Back at Lockwood, Adam told Marcus that Salazar had things under control. The house was secure, and he'd double-checked everything. "It should be good. But I'm a little concerned about Salazar. He didn't look good at all—like he had the flu or something."

"Do you think we need to get someone else to cover for him?"

"Not now," Adam replied. "He knows the house, and Dr. Jefferson seems comfortable with him. We should remember to check on him later though."

Marcus pulled a quarter from his pocket. "Let's flip for who gets the Bunkhouse first. Heads or tails?"

Adam called heads, and it came up heads. But he told Marcus, "You can take the first shift. Sweet dreams, brother. I'll get you up in three or four hours."

Marcus left for the Bunkhouse, and after checking in with Piper and Tracy, Adam downloaded the security app onto his desktop and the desk sergeant's computer. They could now monitor both interior as well as exterior cameras covering Jefferson's house. The rest of the night was uneventful, as the two detectives took turns catching some well-deserved sleep.
~~~~

CHAPTER THIRTEEN

TERRY BLACKWOOD'S OLD Chevy Cavalier was parked under the Limehouse Bridge. Adam pulled up, and Terry got in the backseat. Marcus tossed him a sandwich he'd picked up at Jimmy John's.

"Blackwood, you need to put some meat on those bones of yours. Eat up."

"Thanks. Best offer I've had all week."

"What's the word, Terry?"

"Your guys rocked last night, fan was on fucking high when the shit hit it," he said between bites. "My guys in the Posse are pissed. Nobody saw it coming."

"Any talk about Vicario?" Adam asked.

"Yeah. Whoever planted the word did a nice job. Just like we wanted, talk is that this went down because Vicario hit you guys."

"Good. Is he still solid?"

"He is. At least for the time being. But if you keep the pressure on, who knows? Nobody wants to mess with the SWAT boys."

Adam winked. "Don't worry, there's more in the pipeline. We're bringing in Moreno next. That should shake things up big time. Keep your ears to the street and let us know what's up."

"Will do," Terry said. "And next time make the sandwich a veggie. I need to keep my girlish figure."

~~~~

Back at the station, they met Boyer and Merchant and told them that the plan to undermine Lucas Vicario's leadership seemed to be working. Chief Merchant instructed Boyer to keep the pressure on but to make sure it remained under control.

"Don't worry, Chief," Boyer gloated. "I've got it covered."

Later that afternoon, Officer Salazar reported that everything went smoothly at Dr. Jefferson's office, and they were back at his house. He had it secured, and they were in for the night.

"Marcus, we've got another long night in front of us," Adam said. "You haven't seen Makayla in a few days now. I say go home and spent an hour or two with her. When you get back, I'll do the same with Piper and Tracy."
~~~~

The short time away from the station was time well spent for both of them. Adam returned a shade after 10:00, and they settled in for the night taking turns monitoring the security video of Dr. Jefferson's home and working the murder books.

~~~~

The night was as pitch black as the clothes the man wore.

The Spectra scope was positioned on a tripod behind the gazebo, giving the laser an unencumbered line of sight to the security camera at the rear of the house. He removed the Beretta 71 and secured the suppressor to the revolver. He connected the portable power supply and activated the blue beam for two seconds searing the sensor and completely disabling the camera. The tripod, scope, laser, and power supply were disassembled and packed in a black duffle bag thirty seconds later.

Adam was watching the quadrants from Jefferson's home on his computer monitor, each showing perfect inactivity in night-vision's ghostly greenish hues. He'd just set his coffee down when one quadrant went completely dark.

"Shit," he muttered and tapped the side of the monitor—even though he knew it wasn't going to do a thing. In his gut, he knew Jefferson was in trouble. "Marcus, we got a problem."

Marcus saw the dark quadrant and immediately called dispatch. He gave the operator Jefferson's address, and ordered a unit sent out to his house.

Adam was already on his cell phone calling Salazar.
~~~~

The phone rang six times before a sleepy voice answered, "Yes."

"Salazar, wake up! It's Stone"

Still somewhat confused, Salazar said, "Detective Stone?"

"Listen to me," Adam said, "I just lost the rear camera. I need you to confirm."

Salazar glanced at the computer on the table next to the couch where he'd fallen asleep. "Confirmed, sir. I only see three."

"Where's Jefferson?"

"Asleep."

"Okay. I need you to get him up," Adam ordered.

A moment later, Salazar was back on the line. "He's here with me, sir."

"Okay, listen carefully," Adam said. "I want you to take Dr. Jefferson with you and check to make sure all doors and windows remain closed and locked. Then I need you to get a visual of the back of the house." A few moments later, Salazar was back on the phone. "I'm at the dining room window but can't see much of anything, sir."

"Do you have your bodycam and an earpiece?"

"Yes, sir."

"Good. I need you to put them on and recon the rear of the house, but have Jefferson lock the door behind you when you exit. Understood?"

"Yes, sir." Adam could hear footsteps and then muffle voices. Salazar held his gun in a right-handed front ready position—a high intensity flashlight in his left hand positioned over his right wrist in an "ice pick" grip. "I'm exiting the front door."

Adam again heard steps and background rustling. "Where are you now?"

"At the right rear corner of the house." He moved forward slowly arcing his gun and flashlight back and forth. He surveilled the rear of the house—the beam of the flashlight sweeping across the pool, lawn, and gazebo. Nothing. He trained the flashlight on the security camera but could see no physical damage. He then backed up to the front door and knocked. Jefferson quickly unlocked the door and Salazar slipped in.

He was breathing hard and sweating when he removed the bodycam and said, "Back inside. Everything looks clear. Maybe the camera broke or something."

"Hell of a strange time for a camera to break," Adam quickly replied. "We've got officers on their way out there. Stay by your phone and call me as soon as the officers arrive."

Lying behind a five-foot privet hedge that ran the length of the yard, the man listened intently but didn't move. He saw the white light cutting back and forth through the blackness. Finally, the light disappeared, and he heard a door close. He silently cursed himself. It was not like him to fail at an assignment. His watch read 4:30 a.m. He rolled from behind the hedge and vanished into the darkness. He had failed, but options remained.

CHAPTER FOURTEEN

"I DON'T BELIEVE in coincidences," Marcus said. "No way did that camera just happen to malfunction in the middle of the night. Someone disabled it. Thank God, Salazar was out there."

Adam glanced at his watch. "The officers should be there by now. We need to get the security company out there."

They made it out to Jefferson's house a half-hour later. Salazar and the doctor were in the living room along with two officers when they arrived. It was still dark, and Adam and Marcus made a cursory check around the perimeter of the house.

At first light, they began a more thorough investigation. There was no visible damage to the security camera itself, and they began working their way around the pool and across the lawn toward the river.

"Adam, over here," Marcus said pointing to a spot on the ground behind the gazebo. "See those footprints? Now look to the right." There were three clear indentations in the dirt. "They look fresh." Marcus bent down for a closer look. "What do you make of these?"

"Don't really know," Adam answered. "Maybe a stool or chair?"

"I'll call the station and get techs out here" Adam said. "We'll also need photos and casts of the footprints. I'll lay money they'll match what we found behind Dr. Morgan's house."

Adam was about to comment when the ADT van turned into the driveway. After introducing themselves to the technician, they walked to where they could get a view of the camera.

"It went out in the middle of the night." Adam said. "We can't see any damage. Go ahead and see if you can figure out what happened."

"No problem. I'll get my tools and ladder and be right back."

The technician returned and extended his ladder to reach the camera, mounted about fifteen feet up. He scaled the rungs and removed a voltage meter from his tool belt—the device was still receiving power. He then unscrewed the lens cover and peered inside. A moment later, he was back on the ground.

"What do you think?" Adam asked.

"You've got a burnt sensor."

"What's that mean?"

"It's a bit more complicated, but in simple terms a sensor is a solid-state device that captures the light required to form a digital image. In this case, the sensor looks like it was fried. The camera is still getting power, which means there probably wouldn't have been a power surge—otherwise, the other cameras would have been blown."

"What could have done that?"

"You can 'blind' a security camera by focusing a bright light at the sensor, but that would just blur the image. In this case, the sensor itself was cooked. If it didn't burn out on its own, I'd say it was most likely hit with a laser. You see that sometimes when people take pictures at rock concerts. Their camera can be temporarily disabled if it gets hit by one of those lasers used in the show. But if a laser was used here, it would have to have been a fairly powerful one to fry that sensor."

Both detectives turned back and looked at the gazebo.

"Follow us," Adam said. They walked back, and Adam guided the technician toward the three indentations. "Could someone have used a laser from here to disable the camera?"

"Sure," he replied. "You got a clear shot. No problem as long as the laser had enough power. You'd also need to focus the beam for a second or two. Looks like those marks might be from a tripod. That could've done the trick."

"Thanks," Adam said. "It looks like that's what must have happened."

"Glad I could help. Do you want me to replace the sensor?"

"Not yet. CSI will be here shortly. I'd like you to talk to them first. But while you're here, go ahead and check the rest of the system to make sure everything else is working correctly."

"No problem with that, sir."

Adam and Marcus knew the importance of Dr. Jefferson going into his office and treating his patients like he normally would. They were both convinced that the Sandman, or whoever was at Jefferson's house that night, would try again. Shadowing Jefferson while he continued his practice still presented the best opportunity to catch the killer.

Back inside the house, Adam reassured Jefferson that officers would be with him both at work and at his house. "Officer Salazar will be with you the entire day. We'll finish up here and make sure the security system is working correctly. In addition to Officer Salazar, I'm going to try to have another officer at the house tonight."

Before Adam and Marcus left, Dr. Jefferson pulled them aside. "I wanted to let you know Officer Salazar is in pretty bad shape. I figured he wouldn't say anything, but the poor guy's really sick. He was up most of the night throwing up."

Adam agreed and told Jefferson they'd get another officer out to his office to cover for him.

Adam had the two officers remain at the house to make sure the security system was in working order, and everything was locked up after forensics finished their work.

~~~~
~~~~

After giving Boyer a recap of what had happened at the doctor's house, Adam explained that Salazar was ill and in no condition to continue to guard Jefferson.

"Frank, trust me, you need to get another officer to cover the doctor."

"Sorry guys, but no can do," Boyer replied. "You heard Merchant. Operation Blackout could go down any time now. I hear what you're saying, but I'm the one who has to make the tough decisions. It's your investigation, and that means you're going to have to take care of your doctor yourselves."

Fed up with Boyer but realizing there wasn't much they could do about it, they left for Merchant's office.

"Is the chief in?" Marcus asked his secretary.

"Yes. Have a seat, and I'll check if he's available."

A few minutes later, Merchant opened his door and waved them in. "I hear you two had quite a night. Let's hear it."

After a quick review of the night's events, Adam said, "Chief, we've uncovered a lot of information on these cases. All three crime scenes match the MO of this Sandman character, but apparently no one actually knows who he is except Salvatore DeLaurentis, the boss of the Chicago Outfit and his underboss, Emilio Cataudella. There's no doubt that Nick Santoro was aware of the murders of Richardson and the other doctors. We did find one link between Nick Santoro and Dr. Richardson—Liam Burns. He's one of Santoro's bodyguards and had visited Richardson a few times shortly before he was murdered. We've held off bringing him in because we didn't want Santoro to know we ID'ed him. We think it's time to get him in here and see if we can shake something loose."

Merchant pointed to his office door. "Shut it." Marcus did, and the chief continued, "We're about to do just that, detectives. I spoke to Agent Franco this morning. Operation Blackout is scheduled to go live in all target cities either tonight or tomorrow night. Franco is coordinating our part in the operation with DEA, Captain Boyer, and Chito's SWAT Team as we speak."

"What part will we play in this?" questioned Marcus.

"That's up to Boyer. it's Frank's call on this one."

They left Merchant and headed right back to Boyer's office to plead their case—and suck up if they had to. "Listen, Frank," Marcus began, "Officer Salazar is sick as a dog. No way is he in any shape to take care of Dr. Jefferson. We know you've got your hands full, but we really need you to shake lose an officer to cover Jefferson. We know the operation's going down tonight or tomorrow night, and we need to be part of this thing."

"Who told you that?"

"The chief," Marcus answered.

"Damn it. I'm running this operation. I already told you I need you to take care of your own investigation. It's been almost a week, and the killer is still out there. Now, get out there and do your job."

"Yes, sir," Adam said in a mocking tone. "You're the captain. I just wish you'd start acting like one."

"Stone, nobody talks to me like that! You will …"

They were already leaving Boyer's office, tuning out the rants from the red-faced captain.

Their frustration was evident when they got back to their desks. "Like it or not, we're going to have to cover Jefferson ourselves," Marcus said. "You can take the first shift, and I'll be out there around 1:00 p.m. to relieve you. Not much else we can do now. We'll just have to wait and see what happens with the FBI raids."

When Adam arrived at Jefferson's office, it was clear Salazar's condition had worsened. He was as pale as a ghost. Adam walked him to his car and said, "Get yourself home, Dennis. We've got this."

"I'm sorry, sir. I don't want to let you down."

"You're not letting anyone down. Now, go home and get some rest. You're a good cop."

Adam already knew the layout of the office and remembered there was a rear exit at the end of the hallway just past the doctor's personal office. He confirmed it was locked. There were three offices in the hallway—the first two examination rooms and the third Dr. Jefferson's office.

For the next several hours, Adam sat next to the front door. He checked in with Marcus every hour and made calls to Terry Blackwood and Chester Wood to see if they'd heard anything new on the three murders or Vicario's situation. He observed nothing he considered out of the ordinary that morning. Finally, Marcus showed up to relieve him.

A fairly steady flow of patients were in and out that afternoon. And toward the end of the day, an older gentleman ambled in. Marcus checked his watch and assumed it would be the doctor's last patient of the day. The bearded man used a cane and was hunched over as he haltingly walked to the sliding window. He removed his Clemson ballcap and bent down even more when he spoke to Mary Akerman.

"Hello, my dear," his voice frail. "I'm Stanley Willard. I have an appointment with the doctor."

"Yes, Mr. Willard," Mary said. "I'll need your driver's license and insurance cards." The old man fumbled with his wallet—finally passing the cards through the glass opening. She smiled and handed him a clipboard with a few forms attached. "Please fill out these papers and give them back when you're finished."

The man took the forms, shuffled to a chair against the far wall, and sat down. He put on a pair of wire-rimmed glasses and began working on the forms. A few moments later, a young woman walked out of the hallway door leading to the examination rooms, spoke briefly with Mary, and left the office. Shortly after, the old man returned to the window and passed her the completed forms.

"You'll want to check those, dear. I don't see very well anymore." He smiled at her. "It's not easy getting old."

Mary returned the smile. "Thank you, Mr. Willard. Please have a seat. I'll be right out to take you back to see the doctor."

The man smiled and nodded at Marcus on his way back to his seat.

A few moments later, Mary appeared at the hallway door. "Right this way, Mr. Willard."

The old man stood and made his way to the doorway. As Mary was shutting the door, she turned back to Marcus and whispered, "He's our last patient."

Marcus watched the man leave the waiting room and pulled out his cell phone to let Adam know he'd be wrapping up shortly.

Mary had just returned to her desk when it suddenly occurred to Marcus that the old man had no longer been stooped over as he walked down the hallway. His head swung back to where the old man had been seated. The cane was there!

Then it hit him. *The Sandman!*

Marcus was out of his chair and through the doorway seconds later but froze when he saw the old man spin around holding a Beretta 71. The man was at the end of the hallway just outside Dr. Jefferson's office—a good twenty-five feet from where Marcus stood.

Marcus reached for his shoulder holster, but it was too late. The bullet slammed into his left shoulder spinning him around. He hit the floor hard and looked up in time to see the Beretta's long suppressor pointed at him. He rolled to his right just as a second and third shot were fired. They missed him by inches—ricocheting off the tile floor and splintering the reception room door.

Marcus pulled out his Glock and rolled back into the hallway. He got off a shot but missed high and to the right. The old man fired again. The bullet caught Marcus in his right forearm—the Glock flew from his hand. Marcus was now exposed and an easy target. But before the old man could pull the trigger, his head snapped back. He hit the wall and slid to the floor. Marcus was on his feet, retrieved his gun, and scrambled down the hallway to the old man. He kicked the Beretta away and shot a look through the door to his right. Dr. Ron Jefferson was standing behind his office desk—holding a .22 Mark IV Ruger target pistol. The expression on his face displaying a strange mix of virulence and disbelief.

The bullet had hit the side of the man's head—tearing off the top part of his right ear. He was bleeding profusely and seemed stunned and semiconscious. By now, Jefferson was at Marcus' side and noticed his torn sleeve and the blood dripping from beneath his windbreaker. He started to say something, but Marcus cut him off and yelled, "911! Call 911!"

Marcus holstered his gun and reached around his back for his cuffs. Suddenly, the old man's eyes opened. He pulled his right leg back and snapped it forward—catching Marcus full force in his face. His nose cracked and he tumbled backward unconscious. Jefferson was stunned by the speed and violence of the blow. Then his eyes caught sight of the Beretta on the floor about ten feet away. He froze for a second—giving the old man time to scramble to his gun, roll over, and fire.

The bullet hit Jefferson in the chest, the impact of the projectile immediately dropping him to the floor. The man was now back on his feet and standing over the doctor. He reached into his pocket, removed a small amount of sand, and pointed the Beretta at the center of Jefferson's head. He pulled the trigger. The gun made a metallic click.

"Fuck," the man muttered realizing he'd fired all six bullets.

His head and ear were still bleeding badly, and he was feeling lightheaded—his eyesight beginning to blur. His head swiveled to his right, and he caught sight of Marcus beginning to move. He thought for a moment before he stumbled down the hallway to the rear exit and left the building.

Marcus' eyes fluttered open. He was confused until the coppery taste in his mouth and the searing pain in his nose and left shoulder snapped him back to reality. He saw Jefferson sprawled out on the floor to his right bleeding from his chest. The door to the rear exit was wide open. He managed to remove his cell phone and dial 911. His left arm was useless, and he put the phone on speaker and used his right hand to apply pressure to Jefferson's wound.

As soon as the operator answered, Marcus shouted, "This is Detective Williams! I've got a 10-45c! Multiple victims! Location—Daniel Island—Clements Ferry Road—Office of Dr. Ronald Jefferson! Suspect at large! Need backup! Now!"

The first police car arrived less than three minutes later. Officers entered the building; their guns drawn shouting, "Police! Police!"

Marcus called out to them, and they made their way down the hallway, clearing each room as they went. Still hyped from the adrenaline rush, Marcus took control. He ordered one officer to take over applying pressure to Jefferson's wound and the other to check the area outside the rear exit. Marcus started to give the first officer a cursory review of what had happened when he stopped mid-sentence. "Mary! Where's Mary?"

He made his way back up the hallway and into the room behind the sliding glass window. He heard a whimpering cry and found her trembling and hyperventilating under her desk. She looked on the verge of going into shock. Two more police cars arrived, and the officers began securing the area and attending to Dr. Jefferson, Mary, and Marcus until the paramedics and two ambulances made it to the scene.

A few minutes later, Dr. Jefferson was on a gurney being wheeled through the reception room and into one of the ambulances. He was now conscious—his wound sealed, and the bleeding controlled by a chest compression bandage.

Marcus was seated in the reception room holding a towel over his broken nose. A paramedic was attending to his shoulder when he happened to look to his right and saw the cane. He called out to one of the CSI techs and told her to dust for prints and secure the cane in an evidence bag.

"I need you to get that cane to Lockwood now. Have one of the technicians run the prints as soon as you get there. Make sure they call me when the scan is complete!"

Marcus was about to phone the station when Adam burst through the front door. He took in the scene and went directly to Marcus whose right hand was now holding a towel against his left shoulder and his left hand trying to stem the bleeding from his broken nose.

"Jesus, Marcus," was all Adam could say.

A slight smile appeared on Marcus' face. "Interesting afternoon."

"What the hell happened?"

The smile disappeared and Marcus said, "Sorry, partner. I messed up big time."

"Forget it, brother. We'll deal with it."

Marcus had just started to describe what happened when Adam interrupted. "Wait a minute. You're saying you saw the guy? What'd he look like?"

"Tall," Marcus said. "Fairly long gray hair and a beard. I don't know about the hair, but the beard was fake. Part of it came off when Jefferson shot him. No doubt he was old, but he sure as hell moved like he was much younger."

"Wait a minute," Adam said, his face a combination of surprise and confusion. "You said Jefferson shot the guy?"

Marcus went on to describe how the events transpired— leading to the old man getting away through the rear exit.

"Looks like you got your nose rearranged. How's the shoulder?" Adam asked.

"Not the first time my nose got broken. Don't think the shoulder's too bad. Hurts like hell, but I think it's just a flesh wound." Marcus' eyes glassed over, and he muttered, "Hey, partner, I'm feeling a little woozy."

The adrenaline high was subsiding, and Adam could see that the color had drained from Marcus' face and he was sweating. He called out to one of the paramedics and told him to get Marcus to the hospital.

"Wait a second," Marcus said. "The old man came to the office with a cane but left it in the reception room. I had one of the techs dust it for prints. She's on her way downtown to have them run. You'll need to follow up on that."

"I'll do that. Now we need to get your ass to the hospital. I'll get down there as soon as I finish up here. You did all right, brother."

CHAPTER FIFTEEN

ADAM PHONED MAKAYLA and let her know Marcus had been shot but assured her his injuries were minor.

"God, Adam. What happened?"

Adam gave her a quick recap. "You go ahead, and I'll see you at the hospital as soon as I'm finished here."

Makayla had seemed subdued on the phone call, but he could tell that Marcus was going to be discussing retirement again with her soon.

For the next hour, Adam assumed control of the crime scene. Mary Akerman was still shaken but agreed to stay long enough to help Adam retrieve the visuals from the building's security cameras. The cameras were motion activated, and the one covering the parking lot and main entrance showed an older man exiting a late model Chevrolet Impala at 4:28 that afternoon. He walked to the front entrance using a cane.

The same man was seen running to the Impala holding the side of his head at 5:18. He ran with a noticeable limp. One of the interior cameras covered the reception room. There was also one positioned to view down the hallway and rear exit door. It recorded the entire sequence of events involving the old man, Dr. Jefferson, and Marcus. Adam had Mary make copies before she left. Knowing the old man was at large, he ordered an officer to follow her home and cover her until he was relieved.

Forensics was still working the scene when Adam left for the hospital.

He found Makayla waiting in the emergency room. After a hug, Adam asked, "How's he doing?"

"The doctor said he'll be okay. They took X-rays to make sure the bullet didn't hit his heart or lungs." She glanced at her watch. "He should be discharged any time now. Adam, this is two times in the last year. I'm not sure how much longer I can take it."

He was about to answer when Marcus and his doctor walked into the waiting room. Marcus was wearing the top half of medical scrubs—his arm in a sling and his nose and right forearm heavily bandaged.

He hugged Makayla gingerly and said, "I'm all patched up, babe. The doc took good care of me."

The doctor nodded at Adam and approached Makayla. "Mrs. Williams, I'm Dr. White. Your husband's going to be fine. I removed the bullet and found no substantive damage to any organs or major muscles. The sutures should come out in about ten days, and he'll need to take it easy for the next several weeks. I've given him a prescription if he needs something for pain. All things considered, he should recover completely in the next month or so."

"Thank you," Makayla said. "We'll take good care of him."

"How's Dr. Jefferson?" Adam asked.

"He's out of surgery and in the ICU. He lost a lot of blood but was lucky. The bullet was a small caliber and hit one of his ribs which deflected it away from his left lung. I've already spoken to Mrs. Jefferson, and she'll be here later this evening."

"That's great news," Adam said.

They weren't even through the emergency room doors before Marcus asked for an update. Adam told him about the security cameras and assured him the prints from the cane were being processed. "I'm heading over to the station now. You've done enough for one day, partner. Get yourself home and do everything Makayla tells you to do."

Marcus smiled. "I always do. Do you think that old guy is the Sandman?"

"Who knows? Maybe we'll luck out with those prints. I'll let you know what we get. Now, enough talk. Go home. I'll see your ass tomorrow."

~~~~

Adam went directly to Merchant's office and was waved in by his secretary. He gave the chief an update on what had transpired that afternoon at Dr. Jefferson's office and Marcus' condition. "Chief, our suspect is hurt, but he's still
~~~~

out there somewhere. Jefferson should be out of the ICU shortly and moved to a private room. I'd like an officer stationed outside that room."

"All right, Adam. I'll assign Cummings. Frank won't be happy you went around him, but I'll deal with it."

"Thank you, sir. Where do we stand on Operation Blackout?"

"We're still on standby waiting for orders from Chicago to move on Santoro's organization." He glanced at the clock and continued, "It's almost 9:00. I doubt anything will happen tonight."

Adam thanked the chief and left for forensics' biometric department to check on the prints.

Max Muller was the imaging technician on duty, and Adam asked if he'd had any luck with the prints from the Jefferson crime scene.

"Yeah, but this is strange. It looked like someone tried to wipe down the cane, but I did find one slap image with a NFIQ score of 1 and another with a 2. I ran the scans, and there's no doubt who those prints belonged to."

"I need a name, Max!"

"Walter Cobb," Muller answered. He picked up a sheet of paper from his desk and continued, "The hit came from an old Chicago Army enlistment database back on June 12, 1967. The weird thing is that it was the only print match I got—nothing after that. There's no doubt this Cobb fellow enlisted in the army back in '67, but in the early 90s, the dude disappeared. Couldn't find anything after that."

"That's crazy," Adam said. "How does somebody stay under the radar for over 30 years?"

"Got me," Muller replied.

"What else did you get from the scans?"

"Not much. Cobb was born on December 5, 1948. His home address was listed in South Chicago. Got his social security number, but that's about it." Muller handed Adam a computer printout. "Everything's on the printout."

"All right, stay with it. Maybe something else will pop up."

Adam hurried back to his desk and called Steve Gagyi. He was at his girlfriend's apartment but immediately agreed to come into the station.

While waiting for Gagyi, Adam checked all the hospitals and urgent care clinics to see if a Walter Cobb or Stanley Willard had been treated. No luck. Thinking the old man might have even tried a veterinarian, he called the four vet clinics that were still open. No luck there either. To add to his frustration, he struck out with all the rental car agencies.

Gagyi showed up a half hour later, and Adam gave him what little he had on Walter Cobb. "Looks like he was 18 years old when he enlisted in the Army, lived in Chicago, and most likely wasn't in school. The war in Vietnam was heating up back then and so were the protests." Adam gave Gagyi the printout he received from Muller. "I know it's not much but see what you can dig up on him."

A little over an hour later, Adam got a call from Gagyi. "I've got a few things, sir. Are you available?"

"Hell yes! Come on over."

Gagyi showed up a few minutes later with a sheet full of notes. "We know he was born in 1948—which would make him 71 years old. Army records show he served six years in Vietnam as an Army Ranger and received an honorable discharge in early 1973. No marriage certificate on file in Cook County. Records show he did file his federal and state income taxes until 1992. But that was the last year he filed. After that I ran into a brick wall—couldn't find anything, no employment records, no driver's licenses, no bank records, no credit cards— nothing! It's like he just disappeared."

"Shit," Adam mumbled.

"Wait, there's more. So, I'm about to give up when I decided to run a search of U. S. passport applications in 1992. Bingo, I found that a Walter Henry Cobb applied for a passport that year. There's a section on the application asking what countries the applicant is planning to visit. Cobb put down Costa Rica. Here's where it gets interesting. Costa Rica is like the States—you can search property records."

Adam's excitement was building. "Tell me you found something."

"I did. Records show a Walter Cobb bought a house in 1993 a few miles outside of a small town on the country's western coast by the name of Quepos."

Gagyi used Adam's computer to log into Google Earth and pulled up a satellite picture of Quepos. It appeared to be a medium-sized fishing town with several marinas.

Adam was quiet for a moment—trying to digest the fact that they might have actually found the Sandman. It made sense.

Walter Cobb disappeared in 1992, about the same time the Chicago mob boss, Tony Accardo, gave the order to eliminate Tommy Spilotro in Las Vegas. That was the first time a mob contract killing was attributed to the mysterious Sandman.

"What do you want to do now?" Gagyi asked.

"Cobb's hurt, and now he knows we can identify him. I want you to check the manifests for all the flights out of Charleston to Costa Rica."

"I'll check Chicago too," Gagyi said.

"Good," Adam said. "But we know he's got multiple identifications. He used the name, Stanley Willard, at Dr. Jefferson's office. Check that one too."

Gagyi used his department ID to access the reservation manifests for the airlines flying to San Jose, Costa Rica—United, American, and Jet Blue. Jet Blue had only one flight, and it left daily at 6:15 in the morning. United and American had multiple flights that left at various times between 7:00 a.m. and 4:30 p.m. Neither Walter Cobb nor Stanley Willard appeared on any of the manifests.

"How about flights to Chicago?" Adam said.

Gagyi repeated the process for all the airlines offering flights to O'Hare and Midway. Still no hits. He checked the private charter flying to both Chicago and Costa Rica—nothing.

Adam pulled out the flash drive containing the footage from Jefferson's security cameras. He told Gagyi to find the best visual of Cobb's face and make copies. He would then get them to not only the TSA and airport police, but also to the agents at the local Amtrak and Greyhound terminals.

"In the meantime," Adam said, "I want you to stay on those flights and let me know if either Cobb or Willard show up."

~~~~

A half-hour later, Adam was back in Merchant's office with a hooded but recognizable front and side views of Walter Cobb's face. Merchant was on the phone with Homeland Security and Hank Van Hala; the lieutenant in charge of the Charleston International Airport police. Within an hour, copies of Cobb's photos were in the hands of TSA agents, airport officers, and train and bus agents.

At this point, there wasn't much more Adam could do—it was now a waiting game. The hours dragged on—the hands on the wall clock in the bullpen seemed to be frozen in time. Finally, at 4:15 in the morning, the phone rang. It was Steve Gagyi. "We've got him!"

The name, Stanley Willard, had just appeared on the reservation manifest for Jet Blue's 6:15 a.m. flight bound for San José, Costa Rica with a one hour layover at Miami International Airport.

Adam grabbed his Glock and windbreaker and was out of his seat. "Steve, let Chief Merchant know the Sandman is on the move! He'll advise Van Hala and Homeland. Stay on top of
~~~~

those reservation lists and let me know if anything changes. I'll be at the airport."

Adam could feel the rush of excitement as he left the station. But as he headed to the airport, something felt off—why did the Sandman book the flight using the name, Stanley Willard?

~~~~

The Jet Blue flight to Costa Rica was scheduled to leave at 6:15 a.m. at gate B-6. Shortly after 5:00 that morning, undercover homeland security agents and airport police were stationed in the area around the gate as well as all airport entrances and exits.

People started arriving for the flight, and the waiting area began to fill up. The gate agent initiated the boarding process at 5:45. Still no Sandman. A few stragglers showed up out of breath and were ushered onto the plane. The agent was about to close the gangway door when Adam flashed his badge and stopped her. He entered the plane and walked the aisle—eying each passenger. No Stanley Willard! No Walter Cobb! No Sandman!

Adam's frustration was evident when his cell vibrated. It was Chief Merchant. "Adam, we just got a call from the Greyhound station on Dorchester Road. The agent sold a ticket to a man going to Houston. He said the guy looked exactly like the photo of Cobb we sent to the bus station."
~~~~

"Shit!" Adam said. "Cobb never showed up for the flight. The son-of-a-bitch booked the flight as a diversion—and we bought it! I'll bet he'll fly out of Houston or maybe even stay on the ground all the way to Costa Rica—if that's where he's going. All right, let me think. When did the bus leave?"

"No more than 10 or 15 minutes ago," Merchant replied. "The agent called right after he sold the ticket. He said the bus has a stop in Savannah, but we can get ahold of the driver and have him stop sooner."

"No. That'll spook Cobb. If I leave now, I can beat the bus to Savannah. You know the chief there. Ask him permission for me to deal with Cobb in his jurisdiction. Also, ask him to send officers to the bus station. I'll hook up with them when I get there."

"I'll do it," Merchant said. "Be careful. There's hardly any security at bus terminals, and Cobb will probably be carrying."

"Right. I'll call you from the road."

~~~~

Twenty minutes later, Adam was driving west on I-17 toward Savannah. He called Merchant. "Chief, I need the bus driver's name and cell number. Also how many passengers are on his bus. Can you call him, let him know what's going on, and tell him I'll be contacting him?"

"Can do. I'll get back to you with the information."

"Wait," Adam interrupted. "Ask the chief if I can use two of his best men to board the bus with me."
~~~~

"Will do."

The callback from Merchant came 15 minutes later. Mike Marquard, the Greyhound driver, had been contacted and appraised of the situation. He reported there were only 18 passengers on the bus and confirmed one was the man matching Cobb's description. He was told to expect a call from Stone.

"How about Savannah?" Adam asked.

"I've talked to Chief Wes Clifford. He'll be at the Greyhound terminal with his officers to meet you."

"Good. My ETA at the terminal is 9:05. I'll keep you posted."

Adam hung up and put in a call to the Greyhound's driver. "Mr. Marquard, this is Detective Adam Stone. I know you've spoken to Chief Merchant. Can you talk without being overheard by your passengers?"

"Yes." Marquard's voice was almost a whisper.

"Good. In a few words, describe the passenger you said resembled the photo you saw at the Charleston terminal."

"Over six foot. Older. Longish gray hair. Wearing black jeans and a gray hooded sweatshirt. The hood covered most of his face."

"Where in the bus is he seated?"

"Last row. Next to the left window."

"Good. Now, here's what I need you to do. When you pull into the Savannah terminal, tell your people that a few more passengers will be boarding and to remain seated. Three of us will come on board. I'll have on a red ball cap and be carrying a small backpack. The other two men will also be police officers.

I'll follow the two officers and walk to the rear of the bus. As soon as we have the situation under control, we'll need you to help get the passengers off the bus as quickly as possible without anyone panicking. Say 'yes' if that is clear."

"Yes."

"Good. I'll contact you if anything changes. Call me at this number if you need to. Understood?"

"Yes, sir."

Adam passed the Greyhound bus on I-95 about 30 minutes outside of Savannah and pulled into the terminal a few minutes ahead of schedule. Chief Clifford was waiting and approached Adam as he entered the terminal. "Detective Stone, I'm Wes Clifford." They shook hands, and Clifford nodded toward two officers standing next to him. "Meet Detectives Stark and Carlson. They're the two undercover officers Chief Merchant requested."

Adam shook their hands and explained what he intended to do once the bus arrived. Chief Clifford had all the civilians removed from the boarding area and deployed the rest of his officers around the station. For the next few minutes, the station was deadly quiet until the sound of the bus could be heard as it turned into the station—the high-pitched cry of the air-breaks stopping it in front of the terminal. Approximately 30 seconds later, the bus door swung open, and Mike Marquard stepped out. He nodded once and returned on board.

Stark and Carlson stepped onto the bus followed by Adam. Stark took a seat about a third of the way down the aisle, and Carlson sat down behind the last passenger six rows in front of Cobb. Adam continued until he reached the last row, removed his backpack, and slid in against the right window. He carefully reached into his backpack and removed his Glock—resting it on top of his pack pointed directly at Cobb.

Adam turned toward Cobb and said, "Hello, Walter."

There was no reaction.

He repeated, "Hello. Mr. Cobb—or is it Stanley Willard?"

This brought a slight smile to Cobb's face and he turned and eyed Adam. "Sorry, I think you must be thinking of someone else." Then he saw the Glock. His smile disappeared.

"Now, here's what you're going to do," Adam began. "Slowly place both your hands on the top of the seat in front of you. Make any sudden move, and the first bullet goes into your right thigh. Nod if you understand."

His eyes frozen on Adam, Cobb gave a slight nod and slowly put his hands on the seat in front of him.

"Good. Remove either hand, the next bullet goes into your chest."

Cobb said nothing. It was clear he was considering his options.

"Don't even think about it," Adam whispered. He then called out, "Clear!"

Detective Carlson stood, turned around, and extended his handgun directly at Cobb.

At the same time, Detective Stark and Michael Marquard began directing the passengers off the bus. By this time, Carlson was in the rear of the bus, his handgun still fixed on Cobb.

As soon as the last passenger was safely off, Adam said, "Walter, here's how this is going to go down. We're going to walk off this bus and take a ride back to Charleston. There's a few people who are anxious to talk to you. I want you to slowly stand, face left, and put both hands behind your back." Cobb stared at Adam but didn't move. "Your choice, Walter. Easy or hard."

The smile reappeared, and Cobb slowly turned and put his hands behind him. "Where is your weapon?" Adam asked. Cobb gestured to the overhead bin in front of him. Carlson grabbed the carryon bag, and Adam quickly holstered his gun and removed his handcuffs. After cuffing Cobb, Adam patted him down—removing a wire garrote from his pants pocket and a small black Kershaw knife from an ankle sheath. He put the garrote and knife in his windbreaker. He removed his Glock and pulled off Cobb's hood—exposing a blood-soaked bandage covering what remained of his right ear. "You need to know something. You shot my partner who also happens to be my best friend. Give me the opportunity, and I'm more than happy to return the favor."

Detective Carlson began walking backwards toward the exit—his gun still leveled at Cobb. Adam followed until Cobb reached the front door and stepped off the bus. He looked up and found a semicircle of seven police officers—their guns aimed at him.

Adam exited right behind Cobb and ordered him to drop to his knees. Cobb did as he was told. Chief Clifford pointed to an officer and said, "This is Officer Rapp. He'll drive you and your prisoner back to Charleston. I'll have another officer follow with your car."

Adam removed his car keys and handed them to the chief. "Thank you, sir." He pointed to Cobb. "Chief, no one knows we've got him. We need to keep this under the radar."

"Understood," Clifford replied.

"Thank you, sir. Charleston owes you one."

Clifford smiled. "Glad we could help. I may just ask you folks to pay back the favor someday."

Cobb was escorted to Rapp's patrol car and locked in the rear seat. Before Adam got into the car, he walked over to Detectives Stark and Carlson, shook their hands, and thanked them for their help. He retrieved Cobb's carryon from Carlson and then turned to Mike Marquard. "Well, Mr. Marquard, that was some bus ride. You did yourself proud."

A moment later, Adam was in Rapp's car heading up I-95. He called Merchant, gave him an update on what had transpired and that he'd be back at the station in about two hours. Once he disconnected the call, he shut his eyes. The next thing he knew, Officer Rapp was nudging him awake. "Sir, we should be at your station in about 10 minutes."

CHAPTER SIXTEEN

CHIEF MERCHANT AND two of his officers were
waiting when Rapp pulled his patrol car around the rear of the
Lockwood station. The two officers removed Cobb from the
patrol car and quickly escorted him directly to Conference
Room 1.

Adam left the car, thanked Rapp, and approached
Merchant. He hadn't slept in over 48 hours, and it showed.
"How are you holding up, Adam?"

"I'm all right, Chief. Got some sleep in the car on the way
back here."

"All right. I've got Cobb on the way to Conference Room
1. Officers will stay with him until you get there. I want you
handling the interrogation."

On the way to the conference room, Adam told Merchant
he'd like to have Steve Gagyi in the meeting.

"No Problem," Merchant said.

A few minutes later, Adam and Steve entered the conference room. Cobb was seated in a metal chair—his left arm and leg cuffed to it. The two officers stood against the wall; their arms crossed over their chests. Gagyi took a seat at the end of the conference table. His eyes riveted on Cobb, Adam dismissed the officers and took a seat across from him.

Cobb gave Adam a cursory glance but said nothing.

Adam leaned forward. "You know what I'd really like to know. What happened back in 1992? Man, you just disappeared. How the hell did you do that? All those years. That must be a hell of a story you've got there. I'd love to hear it."

Cobb remained stoic and said nothing.

"Your choice, Walter. You can keep your mouth shut and spend the rest of your life in prison. But you're smart enough to know you won't last long inside."

Cobb said nothing.

"Or we can work together. Let's face it; you're a little fish in a big pond. But you've got information about the big fish that swim there. If I were you, I'd be smart and use it. Help us, and we'll do everything we can to protect you."

Cobb stiffened but still remained silent.

Adam let the silence build until he finally said, "You know what? I'm going to get something to drink. You want anything?"

Adam was about to close the door behind him when Cobb said, "Coffee. Black."

Twenty minutes later, Adam returned with the coffee followed by Chief Merchant and Elaine Stewart. He gave Cobb his coffee and introduced Merchant and Stewart.

It was Stewart who spoke first. "Mr. Cobb, you're going to be charged with the attempted murder of Dr. Johnson, Mary Akerman, and Detective Marcus Williams. In addition, you will be charged with four counts of first degree murder in the deaths of Dr. Charles Richardson, Dr. Samuel Morgan, Ms. Martha Simpson, and Dr. Nathan Bell."

Cobb took a sip of his coffee.

"Without going into the specifics, you need to understand that we have an overwhelming amount of evidence against you. We have your Beretta and have matched the slugs taken from all four murder victims. Security cameras have identified you at several crime scene locations. That being said, both my office and the federal authorities are extremely interested in the individual or individuals who ordered these killings. We're also sure you know that the people who gave those orders won't hesitate to use whatever means available to permanently silence you."

Cobb remained quiet, but it was apparent Stewart's words were starting to have an effect.

Stewart continued, "I have received authority from the U.S. Attorney General's office in Washington to offer you access to the Federal Witness Protection Program. If you would like legal representation, we will supply it. The decision is yours. However, this offer is not open-ended."

Adam had a sour feeling in the pit of his stomach. While he hated to see Cobb go unpunished, he knew the possibility of taking down Chicago's opioid pill distribution business could save countless lives.

Time was critical. Operation Blackout could go live at any time, and whatever intel they got from Cobb could be vital.

Stewart stood. "You have one hour to make your decision. I suggest you take advantage of the opportunity before it disappears."

Stewart turned to Chief Merchant and said, "You can call me with Mr. Cobb's decision."

She was leaving when Cobb called after her, "How will I know the Feds will follow through if I take your offer?" It was clear Cobb wasn't all that impressed with police protection since he had little problem circumventing it.

Stewart turned around. "As long as you give us the name or names of who ordered the murders of Charles Richardson, Samuel Morgan, Nathan Bell, and Ronald Jefferson and your testimony is verifiable, the U.S. Attorney General's office will specify the parameters of the offer in writing. As I said, you are free to hire an attorney, or we can supply one. However, this needs to be done now."

"I have an attorney. Before I agree to anything, I'll need to speak with him."

Adam was surprised Cobb seemed willing to cooperate. Then again, Cobb knew he was now a liability to Chicago and had simply run out of options.

Just as Adam retrieved a phone from the far end of the table, the door flew open, and Frank Boyer entered the room.

"So, you got the son-of-a-bitch! No way was he …"

Merchant cut him off. "Frank, that's enough. Not another word!"

Boyer was silenced—stunned by the force in Merchant's voice.

Adam turned back to Cobb who gave him a number with a 312 area code. Adam dialed and passed the phone to Cobb, and for the next few minutes, Cobb quietly spoke to his lawyer, Anthony DeSantis. He then gave the phone to Elaine Stewart, and she listened as DeSantis requested a signed affidavit identifying the U.S. government's intent to assign his client to the Federal Witness Protection Program. Stewart agreed and told Cobb's lawyer the affidavit would be sent to him within the hour.

"We'll be back as soon as your attorney approves the document. Once you sign it, we will need to take your statement." Cobb nodded his agreement. Adam remained by the door after Stewart, Merchant, and Gagyi left the room.

"Walter, tell me something," Adam asked. "Are you the Sandman?"

A foreboding smile appeared on Cobb's face, but he again said nothing.

CHAPTER SEVENTEEN

AFTER A BIT of back and forth with Anthony DeSantis, the affidavit was finalized. Cobb signed the document and sat back, settling a gaze on Adam that about sent a chill up his spine. Adam could see a hint of it—the glee Cobb took in finally being able to accept his ruin. Adam hit the record button, gave the time and date, and identified himself and the other individuals present.

"Mr. Cobb, we understand you served as a Ranger in the U.S. Army until you were discharged in 1973. What did you do after you left the service?"

For the next twenty minutes, Walter Cobb described his job as a travelling welder for several steel mills and iron foundries in Chicago and western Indiana. In the 1980s, many of the large mills around Chicago began to close down, and work was hard to find. For the next several years, he was forced to work a variety of odd jobs.

"I see," Adam said. "When did you become involved with the Chicago Outfit?"

"I spent my last tour in Nam with another guy from South Chicago named Joe DiNapoli. Joe's dad was a bagman for the Outfit. Joe and I started doing some collecting for his dad when we were discharged, and I got to know some of the local wise guys. I used to do some jobs for them after I started working at the mills."

"Excuse me," Elaine Stewart interrupted, "What do you mean by 'jobs?'"

"Sometimes, people would ask me to convince someone to do something."

"Did these people ever instruct you to kill someone?"

"From time to time, people would ask me to remove a problem for them."

"And did you ever remove a problem? Did you kill on command? Just a yes or no answer."

"Yes."

"Did any of those orders to kill come directly from Anthony Accardo, Salvatore DeLaurentis, Emilio Cataudella, or Mr. Edward Santoro?"

"I did some jobs like that for Accardo, DeLaurentis, and Cataudella starting in the 90s. Never got a direct order from Santoro."

"I want to confirm that you were ordered personally by Anthony Accardo, Salvatore DeLaurentis, and Emilio Cataudella to kill specific individuals. Is that true?"

"Yes."

"And were there other contract killings you carried out during the 1970s and 1980s?" Stewart asked.

"There were some, yes. But not for the Outfit."

"I see. Did you ever become an associate or a formal member of the organization called the Outfit?"

"No, I did not," Cobb answered.

"Would I be correct in assuming you were ordered to carry out the killing of more than five individuals?"

"Yes."

"More than ten individuals?"

"Yes."

"More than twenty individuals?"

Cobb shrugged but said nothing.

An eerie silence fell over the group until District Attorney Stewart asked point blank, "Who ordered the killings of Charles Richardson, Samuel Morgan, Nathan Bell, and Ronald Jefferson?"

"Emilio Cataudella."

"All right then. Mr. Cobb, we were unable to find any information on you after 1992. Could you please tell us why that was?"

Walter Cobb said nothing for several moments before speaking.

"I killed a lot of enemy soldiers in Vietnam. We all knew we might die in the war, so we did what was needed to do. The people I killed after the war also knew that they might die because of the life they chose to lead. I figured there wasn't much difference between the gooks in Vietnam and people that were involved with the mob."

A strange smile appeared on Cobb's face as if he was reliving the murders but disappeared quickly.

"I did a job for Tony Accardo out in Vegas in '92. He liked the way I handled it and told me I was only to work for him from then on. I didn't have much choice, but he treated me well enough. He let me leave the country but would call me back if he needed to send a message to one of his enemies."

"I'm assuming that's when you went to Quepos, Costa Rica," Adam said.

Cobb was surprised Adam knew about Quepos but continued, "Yeah, it was a beautiful place and easy to blend in." The same strange smile appeared again, and Cobb said, "There weren't many policía around Quepos, so I was free to do pretty much whatever I wanted."

"What kind of work did you do there?" Adam asked.

"I worked at a marina and had a small charter fishing business."

"And you were called back to the States when Accardo wanted someone eliminated," Steward stated.

"That was the idea. Like I said, I didn't have much of a choice. I did what I was told to do, or I would disappear. And if they find out you've got me …"

Cobb didn't finish, and Adam jumped right in. "As far as we know, your friends from Chicago have no idea we've got you. As long as you continue cooperating, we will do everything we can to keep you safe. Now, can you tell us anything about why you were sent here to kill these doctors?"

"Not really. I only know they'd become a problem for Mr. DeLaurentis and Mr. Cataudella."

"All right," Adam said. "We're going to keep you here at the station. With any luck, Santoro won't find out we've got you for a while. That will give us time to arrange things."

Stewart was about to say something else when there was a knock on the door, and Chief Merchant's secretary entered. "Sir, I need a word with you."

Merchant left his seat and huddled with her. He then turned back to the group. "We're finished here. The rest of you come with me."

They trailed Merchant to his office. Adam hadn't seen him move that fast in a long time, and he had a feeling he knew why. "Ed, what is it?" he asked.

The chief shut the door and said, "Operation Blackout is on for tonight."

CHAPTER EIGHTEEN

"WAIT A MINUTE," Boyer said. "Why wasn't I told about this first?"

"Frank, it's not important. What's important is we've finally got a shot at taking down Nick Santoro and his organization."

"But I'm Agent Franco's official contact," Boyer persisted.

Merchant ignored the comment and continued, "Agent Bradford received word about an hour ago. Chicago's contacted the other eight cities involved in Operation Blackout, and here's what's going to happen. Franco's people have been surveilling Nick Santoro for the past several months, and if his routine holds true, he should be at Duffy's Liquors on the corner of Addison and Hanover tonight. The liquor store has a back room where he meets a few of his associates every Thursday to play poker. Franco says the game starts at around

10:00 and usually goes until around 3:00 in the morning. Santoro always brings two or three bodyguards."

"How's this going down?" Adam asked.

"Chito Walker will assemble his SWAT Team along with FBI and DEA agents at the fire station on King Street, which is less than a mile from Duffy's. The operation is to be coordinated with the other cities and is scheduled to commence at exactly midnight. Franco will have agents watching Santoro, and if for some reason the poker game doesn't happen, we'll have to redress and take him down wherever he is at that time."

Stewart stood to leave. "What do you want to do about Cobb?"

"He's good staying here tonight, but you'll have to coordinate the FBI and U.S. Marshals Service to move him to Chicago. They'll have a safe house up there to keep him under wraps until he testifies." Merchant glanced at his watch. "It's almost 10:00. Frank, I want you and Adam to go to the fire station. Call me with updates. Be safe out there tonight."

~~~~

Two hours later, the SWAT Team pulled to a stop behind a row of cars fifty yards around the corner from Duffy's Liquor. Chito Walker had already reconnoitered the area and identified that one of Santoro's men was stationed outside the entrance.

Walker quickly deployed three officers to cover the rear of the liquor store. Once in place, they reported back to Walker.
~~~~

Walker turned to one of his men. "Jenkins, I need you to neutralize the man out front. Radio me as soon as you've taken him down."

A minute later, Jenkins quietly transmitted that the situation was neutralized.

"All right men, let's move!"

As soon as Walker and his six SWAT officers were assembled in front of the store, they breached the door with a 42 pound Mighty Mouse battering ram.

Two of Santoro's men, seated just outside the backroom smoking cigarettes, were taken completely by surprise. They were quickly subdued, and the team burst into the backroom, Colt AR-15s and Berettas in the front forward position.

Multiple officers yelled, "Freeze! Police! On the floor! Get down! Now! On the fucking floor!"

Playing cards and poker chips flew into the air as one of the men upended the table. He had his hand on his gun but dropped it when the officers fanned out with guns leveled at his chest. Everyone froze. Suddenly the door in the back of the room flew open and Nick Santoro disappeared into the night.

He hesitated, looked to his left and right, and took off—heading to an opening in the fence at the side of the building. He had barely rounded the corner when he heard someone yell, "Caesar! Fass!"

The K-9 officer released his ninety pound German Shepherd, and hearing the German word for "attack," the dog tore after Nick Santoro. Seconds later, Caesar had Santoro down on the ground, his teeth sunk deep into his left leg. The K-9 officer and three SWAT Team members got to Santoro.

"Poost!" Caesar's handler yelled—German for "release the bite." The dog immediately let go of Santoro's leg.

Once Chito's men had Santoro and the rest of his associates subdued and handcuffed, Chito radioed Agent Franco, "We've got Santoro. Situation is under control. Come on in—Mr. Santoro is all yours!"

~~~~

A short time later, six more squad cars and a forensics team were on the scene. Nick Santoro and his crew were loaded into the cars and hauled off to Lockwood.

Merchant and several officers were waiting in the bullpen when Boyer and Adam made it back to the station shortly after 1:00 a.m.

"Hell of a job tonight, men!" Merchant said.

Frank took a step forward. "Thanks, Chief. The SWAT boys helped."

Merchant shot a look at Adam who winked and said, "Yep, Chief. We just couldn't have done it without Frank."

Everyone was jacked from the success of the raid and hung around the station waiting for word from Chicago on how the other cities faired. Finally, around 3:30, Merchant took a call from Agent Bradford—Operation Blackout was a resounding success. Underbosses and several of their associates in six of the other eight cities had been arrested—Cleveland
~~~~

and St. Lewis had somehow been tipped off. The big catch was in Chicago where Salvatore DeLaurentis, Emilio Cataudella, and Edward Santoro were all in custody.

Boyer had left and was in the bullpen pontificating on how he took down Nick Santoro and his "goons"—leaving Adam alone with Merchant.

Cobb was lying on his cot in the conference room but quickly sat up when they entered.

"Mr. Cobb, we just received word from Chicago that DeLaurentis, Cataudella, and Eddie Santoro are in custody."

Cobb nodded once and laid back down.

CHAPTER NINETEEN

OPERATION BLACKOUT CRIPPLED the Outfit's distribution of Chinese oxycodone throughout the Midwest and Southeast. And the U.S. Justice Department began the process of utilizing the RICO statute to initiate sweeping prosecutions of dozens of associates of the Outfit. Based on the expected testimony from Cobb, first degree murder charges were being prepared against Tony Accardo, Salvatore DeLaurentis, and Emilio Cataudella.

Cobb was in custody of the U.S. Marshals Service and sequestered in a Chicago safe house awaiting his testimony linking Anthony Accardo to the 1992 Las Vegas murder of Tommy and Michael Spilotro. Additional charges were in the works for other contract killings ordered by DeLaurentis and Cataudella, as well as the recent murders of Charles Richardson, Samuel Morgan, Martha Simpson, and Nathan Bell.

Adam was in Merchant's office one morning discussing the disposition of the DOJ's murder cases when he asked the chief about the status of Cobb.

"It's my understanding that the U.S. attorneys are attempting to fast-track Cobb's testimony. As soon as he finishes testifying, he'll be turned over to the U.S. Marshals and put in the Witness Protection Program."

"I wonder where they'll send them."

Merchant smiled. "You're guess is as good as mine. But you can rest assured it'll be one of the best kept secrets out there. Hell, the mob already has a price on his head."

"You know, Chief, I get the feeling Cobb won't be able to make it in the program. Some people say that these contract killers get used to the taste of blood and have a tough time washing their hands of it."

Adam was about to say something else when there was a knock on the door, and the Chief's secretary peeked in with a huge smile on her face. "Chief, your 11:00 a.m. appointment is here to see you."

Merchant returned the smile. "All right, you can send them in."

Adam stood and said, "I better leave."

"Sit down, Adam," Merchant said. "I think you might want to stick around for this."

Adam was momentarily confused. Then the door opened, and Marcus and Makayla entered the room.

"Well, look at you," Adam said. "Up and about already. How's the arm?"

"Feeling better, my friend. Makayla's been taking good care of me."

Adam gave Makayla a hug. "You're a strong woman to put up with him." He turned back to Marcus. "I didn't expect you'd be back on the job so soon, partner."

Marcus took hold of Makayla's hand. "Actually, I won't be coming back, Adam. It's time for Makayla and me to move on. I told the chief I wanted you to be here when I turned in my shield. I couldn't have had a better partner or a better friend."

Adam was quiet a moment gathering his emotions. "I guess I knew this was bound to happen, but it'll take some time for me to accept it. I'm not sure what I'll do without you, but I wish nothing but the best for both of you. God knows you've earned it."

Marcus stood, removed his shield, and placed it on the desk in front of Merchant. "Thank you, Chief. It's been an honor to work with you."

Merchant stood and shook Marcus' hand. "Thank you, Detective Williams, but the honor has been mine."

"I suppose I'll have some forms to sign," Marcus said.

"I'll let you get on with that then," Adam said. "Congratulations again, brother. I'll catch you outside when you're finished."

Adam turned to leave, but Chief Merchant said, "Hold on, detective. We're not done here."

Confusion spread across his face. "I beg your pardon, sir."

"I've just received permission to create a new job here on the force. The title of the position is Drug Strike Force Liaison.

It comes with a set of lieutenant bars, and if you want it—it's yours. By the way, I won't take no for an answer. You'll manage all our undercover detectives and be in charge of coordinating the entirety of our narcotic programs and investigations with the FBI, DEA, and Homeland Security. And the best part of the job is you'll have a staff to manage the day to day paperwork. That means you'll be in the field where you belong."

Adam was still shocked. "I don't know what to say, Chief."

"Then just say, 'Thank you, I accept.'"

A smile beamed across Adam's face. "I do have one question and one request."

"And those are?" questioned Merchant.

"I'd like Steve Gagyi to be transferred to my staff."

"Consider it done. Now what's the question?"

"Who do I report to?"

"You can report to Frank if you really want to, but I thought it would be nice if you'd report to me."

"In that case, sir. I accept!"

The chief reached into his bottom desk drawer and removed a fifth of Maker's Mark Private Select. He placed four glasses on his desk and poured two fingers of the amber liquid into each. He raised his glass. "Protect and serve," he said.

"Protect and serve," Adam repeated. He turned toward Marcus and raised his glass. "Here's to my best friend and the finest damn partner a cop could ever have!"

EPILOGUE

A FEW MONTHS later, Adam was in the courtroom when Cobb testified in the murder trials of Tony Accardo, Salvatore DeLaurentis, and Emilio Cataudella. The trial was closed to visitors and his testimony expedited due to multiple death threats made against Walter Cobb.

As soon as Cobb left the stand, Adam and two bailiffs escorted him out of the courtroom to a rear exit of the court-house where a black van was waiting. Twenty minutes later, the van pulled into a vacant warehouse. When Cobb exited the van, two U.S. Marshals ushered him into another van. Just before Walter Cobb entered the second van, he stopped and turned toward Adam and winked. He then raised his right hand, made his fingers in the shape of a gun, and pointed it at Adam. An uncanny smile appeared on his face as he moved his thumb forward as if firing the gun. He quickly entered the van and it disappeared into the late afternoon traffic.

~~~~

Several months later, Adam was at home on a Saturday afternoon rifling through his mail when an envelope caught his eye. The letter was addressed to "Detective Stone" and had no return address. His curiosity piqued, he opened it up.

Dear Detective Stone,

You're a good detective. You also seem like a nice person. I think you can also appreciate that I had no choice but to do those doctors. Plus, to be perfectly honest, I don't think they were very nice people. Right?

I have to admit I'd forgotten how invigorating it was to get back to doing what I do best. It had been a long time since my friends in Chicago called on my services. I did my homework on you and your partner. And to have a couple of top-notch detectives to play with was just icing on the cake.

It's too bad I can't tell you where I am. It would be nice if you were around. The detectives out here aren't very smart. It wasn't as much fun as it was when you and your buddy were chasing me around. I still can't believe I got caught.
~~~~

It's been almost a month or so since I last satisfied that itch I got inside me. I'm getting the feeling I'm going to have to scratch it again very soon.

I've been thinking it would be fun if I let you know when I plan to put someone else asleep—maybe give you some clues. I think that would be fun. Don't you?

Anyway, I've got to go now. Got to do some planning. I will let you know what I come up with.

Sleep tight,
The Sandman

THE MERCY KILLINGS

Available at:

PROLOGUE

North Charleston, SC ... 2010

A LIGHT DRIZZLE spawned a golden-hued glow on the sidewalk under the halo of the streetlamp. The tree limbs bent low as if laboring under the weight of the thick night air. There was a sickening decay about the neighborhood, the smell of garbage and emptiness. A thin veil of dew lay on the windows of Nick's squad car affording him a somewhat ghostly view of the house. His shirt stuck to his back as he shifted weight in the front seat of the unmarked 2004 Crown Vic and glanced at his watch. 2:00 a.m.

Nick Giordano had been a North Charleston police officer for the past seven years, the last four spent with the department's K-9 Unit. It was only the second week of his assignment to the city's new drug task force—code-named *Street Sweeper*—but the late-night hours, stale coffee, and general tedium of surveillance were starting to grind on him.

He had been parked a block from the corner of Remount and Murry watching the small house with its overgrown bushes and weed-covered lawn since about 11:00 that night. The corner house was not believed to be a trap house but rather a location from which a larger drop was being divided for distribution to drug parlors throughout the city. The house had been quiet all night, with no one entering or leaving. Nick's German Shepherd, Max, sat attentively in the backseat of the squad car. Nick turned around, ruffled his dog's ears, and said, "We'll give it another fifteen minutes, Max."

The task force was spread thin that night with multiple stakeouts throughout the known areas of drug activity in North Charleston. In the so-called "War on Drugs," police departments received federal grants based on total arrests rather than a declining crime rate. The department, like many across the country, was playing the numbers game. That this approach simply clogged an already overloaded court system and did little to stem the flow of drugs didn't seem to bother the suits in Washington. They measured the amount of drugs seized, but not whether arrestees were screened for drug addiction. They tallied the number of cases prosecuted, but not whether prosecutors reduced the number of petty crime offenders sent to prison. Despite all this, most police departments were underfunded and understaffed and had little choice other than bow to the demands of the politicians we all elected.

This was the third night Nick and his dog had spent watching the corner house waiting for Luis Ramirez to show.

Ramirez was one of a few upper-level distributors working directly with what was left of the Beltran-Leyva Cartel. While the once-prominent cartel had lost much of its power, it still controlled a major portion of the drugs coming into the Greater Charleston area, as well as a handful of other U.S. cities. A reliable informant indicated that Ramirez had recently been seen visiting the house on multiple occasions.

Nick had just finished off the last of his coffee and was about to call it a night when a black Dodge Charger, headlights turned off, pulled up and quietly rolled to a stop just beyond the house. A hooded man Nick assumed to be Ramirez exited the Charger carrying a large satchel and walked toward the house. Nick grabbed his binoculars and while he couldn't see the man's face, the guy matched Ramirez's physical description. "Max, looks like our boy showed up after all."

Nick called in a Code 8 requesting cover and back-up (no siren/no lights), clipped his control leash to Max's collar, slipped out of the Crown Vic, and remained low behind it. While waiting for backup, a light appeared behind closed shades in a room around the side of the house that Nick assumed to be a bedroom. After a few minutes, another police car appeared on the scene and parked a block away from Nick's squad car. Nick smiled when his good friend Billy Freeman exited the car. Nick and Billy had gone through the Academy together and remained close.

Freeman quietly made his way to the Crown Vic and, crouching next to Nick, whispered, "What's up, Nick?"

Nick gestured to the corner house and said, "Looks like there's a drop going down at that house. Definitely a crack den, smack shack, shooting gallery—whatever you want to call it. We've got intel that makes this location one of Luis Ramirez's main distribution cribs, and a dude just entered the house who matches Ramirez's description. The house has been dark, and I've seen no other activity in or around the place for the last three hours. I say we take it down."

Nick, like several officers on the task force, had been issued a "no-knock warrant," which permitted him to enter the premises without prior warning. Even though he knew he should wait for additional backup, three straight nights of boredom and the excitement of the moment got the better of him, and he went ahead and called in the Code 966, indicating a drug bust was in progress. Nick drew his Glock 21 and headed toward the house with Max and Billy following close behind.

The officers quietly approached the front door, taking positions on either side of the entryway. Nick felt the familiar rush of adrenaline pounding through his body, as his breathing and heart rate increased, and his senses heightened. He took a deep breath, trying to calm himself, then flipped off the safety on his Glock and removed the control leash from Max's collar. As a drug-sniffing dog, Max had been trained to give the "passive alert" of lying down on all fours when he discovered the scent of drugs. As soon as Nick reached the door, his dog caught the scent and immediately dropped. Nick gently tried the doorknob, but it wouldn't budge. He looked at Billy and shook his head. Freeman, an ex-linebacker for the South

Carolina Gamecocks, was six-foot-three and a solid 240. He gave Nick a hand signal indicating he would kick in the door and then follow them in. Freeman mouthed "one, two, three" then shattered the door with his first kick.

Max was instantly up on all fours and charged through the entry followed by Nick and Billy yelling, "Police! Police! Police!" The living room was small and lit only by a shaft of light coming from a partially opened bedroom door. There was no furniture in the living room except for a mattress on the floor pushed up against the far wall. On top of it lay curled the motionless body of a naked woman. Nick, seeing the bedroom door ajar, gave Billy a hand sign indicating he would clear the room and headed in, his Glock raised in a two-handed shooting position. The room was empty with the exception of a table that held a block of cocaine and a box of sandwich bags.

Then everything seemed to happen all at once.

Drawn by the scent of drugs, Max raced directly to the mattress followed by Billy who made a quick two-finger check for a pulse on the woman's neck and called out, "Got a live one here!" Nick made a quick scan of the bedroom, and seeing no one, yelled, "Bedroom clear!" Assuming Ramirez had left through the back door, Nick tore from the bedroom and ran through the kitchen to the rear exit. Just as he burst through the back door, he heard the unmistakable sound of three gunshots coming in rapid succession from inside the house. He whirled around only to see Billy Freeman on the floor, half his face blown away, and Max lying next to him.

"Son of a bitch!" Nick screamed and was in the living room a second later.

As soon as he rounded the corner, he saw the flash. The bullet entered his chest right below his left shoulder and spun him around. The spin became a tumble as a second bullet shattered his right knee. He was losing focus but managed to get off two quick rounds in the direction of the shooter before his world turned black.

Three squad cars arrived minutes later—their blue and red lights creating a carnival of color. The officers quickly secured the perimeter and entered the house. It looked like a war zone. The sharp metallic smell of gunpowder hung in the air. The first officers on the scene had called in a "ten-double-zero," indicating "officer down, all patrols respond." Nick was unconscious, crimson rivers of blood flowing freely from his chest and knee. One of the officers checked Billy for a pulse, even though it was obvious he was dead. Max's lifeless body lay on the floor next to him. One of the shots Nick was able to get off found Ramirez's heart—he was dead before he hit the floor. The naked woman remained passed out on the mattress, oblivious to the death that surrounded her.

When the EMTs arrived, they quickly assessed the situation, making sure Nick's airway was clear and then addressed the chest wound by sealing it off so air wasn't sucked into his chest. After he was stabilized, Nick was transported to MUSC's Level 1 Trauma Center in downtown Charleston.

Nick opened his eyes and blinked several times, allowing his pupils to adjust to the bright overhead lights of the hospital corridor, as he was rolled to the operating room. He was con-fused until the sharp pain in his chest and knee slapped him back to reality.

"Billy?" he whispered.

He felt a hand on his forehead and heard muffled voices in the background. Then the darkness returned.

Nick was in the operating room for over four hours. The cartridges used by Ramirez were 38 Specials. The entry wound in the upper chest was minimal, but the expanding effect of the bullet caused substantial damage upon exiting his back. The damage to his right knee was far worse. The team of surgeons at the Trauma Center was able to save his leg, but the bullet had shattered bone, ligaments, and cartilage.

After surgery, Nick was in and out of consciousness in the ICU for the next several hours. He caught fleeting sounds and images, none of which made sense to him. Finally, he opened his eyes and saw Ed Merchant, captain of the drug task force, and Lieutenant Steve Williams, who headed up his K-9 unit. Their faces were somber. When Nick managed to whisper, "Billy?", both men simply shook their heads. "Max?"

Lieutenant Williams took Nick's hand. "I'm so sorry, Nick."

Nick Giordano shut his eyes. Then came the tears.

CHAPTER TWO

HE OPENED HIS eyes, heart pounding, shirt soaked with perspiration. The nightmares weren't as frequent as they'd been, but when they came, they came hard. Nick rolled his legs over the side of the bed, sat up, and realized he was still fully clothed. His head felt like he'd been hit by a sledgehammer. He covered his eyes from the harsh morning sun and noticed the half-empty bottle of scotch on the nightstand. He grabbed his watch. 6:30 a.m.

The last thing he remembered the night before was leaving the International Lounge on Dorchester Road.

Nick stumbled out of bed and made his way to the kitchen. He set the coffeemaker and headed to the bathroom where he turned the shower on hot and searched the medicine cabinet for aspirin or whatever. He stripped off his foul-smelling clothes and spent the next five minutes in the shower, hoping to wash away what memories he had of the night before. Five aspirin, a hot shower, and two cups of black coffee—each spiked with a healthy shot of whisky—helped Nick settle his demons and kick-start the day. He made the fifteen-minute drive to the North Charleston Police Station's Fraud Division on Rivers Road.

It had been almost a year. Almost a year since his lack of judgment led to the death of his friend and fellow officer, Billy Freeman, and Max; the only dog he'd ever worked with during his four years at the K-9 Unit. That night in North Charleston he had made mistakes that would have been unacceptable even for a rookie fresh from the Academy. He'd asked himself the same questions thousands of times: *"Why didn't I wait for backup? Why didn't I clear the closet?"*

Nick was placed on paid administrative leave during the two-month-long deadly force investigation. The "shooting board" finally determined the shooting to be "with policy," and after he was cleared by the department psychologist, Nick was free to return to duty. He could no longer handle the physical requirements of the K-9 Unit and was transferred to a desk job in the Fraud Division. While the department had deemed him ready, he was, in reality, far from emotionally prepared to handle the day-to-day grind of being back on the job, even relegated to a desk.

The damage to Nick's leg was so severe that two additional surgeries were required to virtually rebuild the entire knee. The prognosis for a physical recovery was good, but it was clear that Nick would never regain the full use of his leg. The pain was a constant reminder of the deaths he considered himself responsible for that night in North Charleston. During the first six months after the surgeries, the pain was intense, especially late at night and early in the morning. He could have opted for pain pills, but as a police officer, he'd witnessed too many lives cut short by opioids, and in a way, he felt like he deserved the pain.

Virtually every city has its "cop bars," where police officers congregate to let their hair down and trade stories. Smokey's on Rivers Road was one of those spots. You could most always find a group of North Charleston's finest relaxing after their shift change. Before the shooting, Nick would had make a practice of stopping by Smokey's for a beer or two about once a week. Those visits stopped after the shooting, but the beers did not. He'd never been much of a drinker, but bottles of scotch and twelve-packs of beer soon began to empty themselves in a day or two, and he would often find himself closing the bars around his one-bedroom apartment on Dorchester Road. Pick your poison.

At first, the drinking helped ease the constant pain in his leg and smooth over the emotional anxiety building inside him. As the months passed, his reliance on those late-night forays into the world of shots and beers escalated, and his interactions with fellow officers decreased. He just couldn't crawl out of his guilt—he was in too deep. On occasion, he'd wake up in the morning unable to recall where he had been the night before. And more than once, he awoke to find himself in the bed of some bat-faced woman whose name escaped him.

The nightmares kept coming, too, and Nick began to call in sick on a far too regular basis—sometimes not even bothering to call when he didn't show. He had been issued two Letters of Reprimand from his department captain. He was losing control, and he knew it. A darkness as thick as pitch surrounded Nick—his mind throwing up memories he couldn't deal with.

Finally, in August of 2011, he came to terms with his downward spiral, realizing he could lose his life if he didn't make a change. Nick loved being a cop, but now it was eating him up. The booze and the guilt were tearing his world apart. He had thought he could somehow honor the memory of Billy Freeman by staying on the force, but it just wasn't working. He needed to get out. And he needed to get out now.

The following week, Nick submitted his formal resignation from the force, packed a bag, and made the two-hour drive up I-26 to his dad's peach farm in Killian, South Carolina. It was time to go home.

ABOUT THE AUTHOR

Geoff Collins holds graduate degrees in business and finance and a master's degree in education. He has held multiple management positions in Fortune 500 companies and was CEO of a Midwest advertising and public relations firm.

After a successful career in business, he taught elementary school for fifteen years. His passion for teaching reading and writing to his students led to a career as an author of both children stories and adult mysteries.

Geoff lives on Johns Island, South Carolina, with his wife, Sally. He has three grown children, Max, Leigh, and KC, and four grandchildren, John, Collin, Cora, and Lily.

OTHER BOOKS BY
GEOFF AND ART COLLINS

NIKKI AND THE TREE KEEPER

"What a wonderful and lovely tale!"

"Nikki is a heart-warming and inspirational story of finding your place in the world."

"Nikki and the Tree Keeper is magical."

"The illustrations are beautiful and add so much to the book."

www.booksbycollins.com

THE CHRISTMAS TOKEN

"The Christmas Token is a heart-warming holiday tale about generosity, memories, and family."

"The artwork in this tender story is superior!"

"The Christmas Token should become a family tradition to read as the Christmas season begins!"

"Excellent!"

"Lovely book! My kids have read it many times over the holidays."

www.booksbycollins.com

THE ADVENTURES OF ARCHIBALD & JOCKABEB

"One of a kind!"

This is the best book EVER!!!!!! Dragons, Indians, horses, evil crows, there is nothing like it! I loved it … can't wait for more adventures to come.

"A majestic tale—*Harry Potter* meets *The Indian in the Cupboard*"

Loved reading these books. I quickly got hooked, dug in, and engaged with the characters. Wonderful stories.

"Rich in vocabulary!"

This book is rich in vocabulary. I can't wait to read all the other Archibald and Jockabeb books!

"Best of the best!"

In the Forest is an outstanding book! The characters are great and help make the wonderful story come together.

"Terrific series of action books!"

www.booksbycollins.com

WHITE CLOUD AND THE GOLDEN CANYON

Excellent Native American tale for children and adults alike.

Wonderful life lessons for all.

Very enjoyable and true to our culture. (Akta Lakota Museum)

www.booksbycollins.com

THE BLACK CREEK MYSTERIES

Alex Foster and Travis Sanders live in a small southern Ohio farm town named Rivers Edge. Their first adventure takes them to the remote desert town of Sunshine, Arizona, where they find themselves in the middle of the Legend of the Apache Death Cave. The following summer, after Alex and Travis graduate from high school, they head to the small fishing town of Black Creek, Maine, for a relaxing vacation before they both head off to college. Their trip becomes anything but relaxing when they discover a mysterious creature in an underwater cave and a network of deadly gunrunners.

www.booksbycollins.com

THE MERCY KILLINGS

"Well Written … Interesting Characters and Plenty of Suspense"

Good mystery with interesting characters and plenty of suspense. A cybersecurity expert is hired to determine if narcotics theft is taking place at Charleston SC hospital and who is behind it. Well written with lots of fascinating details.

"Wonderfully Crafted Story Set in Charleston"

Wonderfully crafted story set in Charleston, SC—great story line and vivid imagery. Collins follows Giordano with insight and honesty. Can't wait for Nick's next adventure.

"A Fast and Exciting Read"

The book was a fast read. It was exciting and held my interest throughout. Hope to see more from this author.

www.booksbycollins.com

THE TOOLS OF THE TRADE

Mario Rossini's Jersey syndicate, the Beltran-Lyve Cartel, and the KKK's Confederate White Knights are all battling for control over Charleston's drug trade. Nick Giordano and his friends once again find themselves entangled in the fight. And this time they may all be targets for the legendary Mafia hitman, Carlos Tucci.

"Another Wild Ride"

Tools of the Trade takes us on another wild ride with Nick Giordano and his crew. Collins, as he did with his previous book in this three-part series (volume three is coming in 2019), deftly weaves on intricate story line that builds to a satisfying, thrilling end. Highly recommend Collins, a writer who deserves a vast readership.

"Excitement and Suspense"

Excitement and suspense as mafia and white supremacists fight over the drug market in Charleston SC. Characters well-developed and interesting story line.

www.booksbycollins.com

SHARK BAIT

Nick Giordano and his friends are drawn into the dark and dangerous world of the Russian mafia. The East Coast Russian mafia boss, Dimitri "The Shark" Pavlov, and his enforcer, Viktor Dudko, are using Charleston's Port Authority terminals for drug smuggling and human trafficking.

"Hopefully More to Come"

In this series, which sadly wraps here with Book Three, Collins found a higher gear with each, serving up a fresh batch of nasty folks for the series' core characters to root out and take down. That the books were set in Charleston only added to their delight. The only rotten aspect here is that this is the last we'll see of Nick Giordano and his pals—that is, unless, this crew comes around for cameos in one of Collins' future works. Hats off!

www.booksbycollins.com

A DEATH IN THE FAMILY

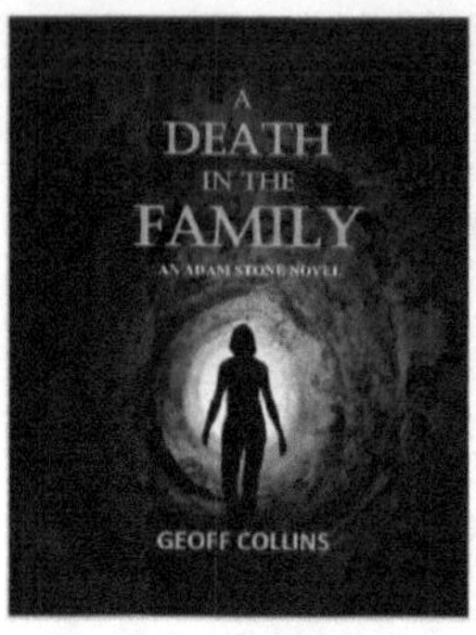

Detective Adam Stone and his partner, Marcus Williams, are part of Charleston's elite Organized Crime Unit investigating a spike in the city's heroin and fentanyl drug trade. During a raid of a major drug distribution house, the shot-caller of the Bloods is shot and killed by Adam. Shortly after that, his wife, Ann, is found murdered. Initially, the Bloods are the obvious suspects. However, as the story unfolds, several other women are murdered, and the list of possible suspects grows. It soon becomes apparent that there is a serial killer roaming the street of Charleston.

www.booksbycollins.com

PRIME SUSPECTS

Prime Suspects is the second in the Adam Stone action-packed murder/mystery series. The dead body of the Joe Wallace, one of Charleston's premier defense attorneys, has just washed up on the shores of the Ashley River. Wallace possessed a dubious reputation as a heavy drinker, gambler, and frequent user of various controlled substances—not to mention his notoriety for chasing skirt. There are no shortage of suspects, and as Adam Stone moves deeper into the investigation, the list continues to grow. One by one, he eliminates the potential killers until he finds himself face to face with the most dangerous of them all … the prime suspect.

www.booksbycollins.com

Reading Partners is a nonprofit literacy organization that recruits and trains community volunteers to provide one-on-one reading tutoring to students in under-resourced schools across the country. This highly effective program has helped thousands of children master the fundamental reading skills they need to succeed in school and beyond. For more information, please visit www.readingpartners.org.

"Literacy is not a luxury; it is a right and a responsibility. If our world is to meet the challenges of the twenty-first century we must harness the energy and creativity of all our citizens."

–President Bill Clinton